AIMEE'S DILEMMA LOVE ME OR LEAVE ME

Tobi Taiwo

*To Martyna and Ellie thank you
for inspiring me to do better.*

Aimee Larkson currently resides at 49 Faircroft Road in Reigate, Surrey England, in a 3-Bedroom semi-detached house with her stepdad Jerome Palmer, her Mum Emma Larkson and her younger brother Tom Larkson. She is in the final year of 6th form education at the age of 17 and maintains a relationship with her boyfriend Matt Morley, her best friend, Kat Casado, and her friend Leyton Stowell who are also 6th formers.

Characters

Aimee Larkson: (17) 6th former in the final year of sixth form; Aimee is in a relationship with Matt Morley.

Emma Larkson: (41) Mother of Aimee; Emma is in a relationship with Aimee's stepdad.

Jerome Palmer: (37) Aimee's stepdad; he has been in a relationship with Emma Larkson for 5 years.

Matt Morley: (17) He is a 6th former in the final year of sixth form; he is Aimee's boyfriend.

Lorraine Morley: (42) She is the parent and mother of Matt.

Kat Casado: (18) 6th former in the final year of sixth form and the best friend of Aimee Larkson.

Leyton Stowell: (18) 6th former; Friend of Aimee Larkson and friend of Kat Casado.

Lucy Stearman: (17) 6th former in the final year of sixth form.

Aiden Stearman: (45) Parent and

father of Lucy Stearman.

NOVEMBER

It was 4:43pm on a cold Tuesday afternoon in November, and Matt and Aimee were spending time together in Matt's bedroom; he lives with his mother in a 4-bedroom detached house at Number 12 Elbury Road in Merstham, Surrey, England.

Matt and Aimee laid next to each other on the double bed, on top of the duvet. It was quiet in the bedroom; they looked into each other's eyes and smiled. Matt was clean shaven, with brown hair and a mid-fade haircut. He is 5 foot 10 in height. Aimee has dark blonde hair in a neat high ponytail and she is 5 foot 8 in height.

Matt moved towards her, kissing her. As they continued to kiss on the bed Matt leaned into Aimee. He was wearing only his grey boxers and she was wearing one of his polo Ralph Lauren t-shirts and her navy-blue skinny jeans. He put his left hand on her cheek as they were kissing and lay on top of her as she put her arms around him. Aimee smiled slightly and as Matt pushed the full weight of his body on her they continued to kiss. Aimee could smell the mint chewing gum on his breath. Matt moved his left hand below her navel then lower down towards the zipper of Aimee jeans. As he pushed his hand into her underwear Aimee told him to stop, shaking her head. Matt proceeded to put his hand further below.

'I said stop!' she said, and Aimee put both her hands on his shoulders and turned her face away from him.

'What are you doing?' he responded. Aimee sat up in the bed putting her back against the pillows, and her head on the headboard she covered herself with the duvet. Matt gave out a sigh and moved away from Aimee - he was now sitting on the bedside,

'Sorry, just not now,' Aimee said with a low voice, then cleared her throat.

'What's wrong?' he responded looking back at her,

'I don't want to at the moment, Matt' she said raising her voice. There was a pause, and Matt swung his fist to the headboard. Aimee gasped. In frustration Matt stood up by the bedside on the opposite side to Aimee and moved towards the bedroom window, whilst letting out a groan. He then bent down to pick up his jeans from the carpeted floor and put them on, 'Matt?' Aimee asked, shocked,

'Just leave, you're pissing me off.'

'Matt I just...' before Aimee could finish, Matt interrupted.

'Get out,' he said, and threw her bag which was on the bedroom floor at her. The bag hit Aimee on the shoulder as she got off the bed. Coming round to the other side of the bed, she stood next to Matt and she laid her hand on his shoulder as he shrugged.

'Not now,' he responded and proceeded to open his phone, completely ignoring her.

'Matt! Look at me!' Aimee said calmy, putting her arms around his waist and facing him. She felt the warmth of his body as she held him, her back to the bedroom window.

Aimee put her forehead on his bare chest then looked up at Matt. 'I just want us to spend time together,' she said.

'And do what?' he replied looking at Aimee straight in the eye. He peeled Aimee's arms from around his waist then continued to scroll through his phone. 'How long is this going to go on for?' he said to her with a frustrated look as he sat back down on the bed.

'I just have a lot on my mind Matt,' Aimee kneeled by the bedside looking up at him. She put her hand on his thigh but Matt shook his head.

'Yes, but you're so needy and boring and what am I getting in return? Just sitting here wasting my time,' he said with bitterness.

'It's not like that - I love you. We've always enjoyed spending time together,' she said, looking perplexed. Matt stood up from the bed and Aimee got up as well as he faced her, putting his hands on her shoulders.

He said, 'You used to be so much fun!' there was a pause and Matt sighed. 'Even the way you dress has changed.'

'Wait, what's that supposed to mean?' Aimee asked.

'Aimee, I can't do this right now this is pointless!' Matt picked up the remote control on the bedside table and he turned on the television mounted on the wall.

Aimee was quiet, surprised by her boyfriend's behaviour. With her mouth slightly open, as she stood by the bedroom window, she could feel the heat of the radiator mounted on the wall against the back of her thigh. She was looking at him as he said nothing back at her.

'Ok, erm,' said Aimee unsure of what had just happened. She looked to the bedroom floor and put her socks and trainers on then said to Matt, 'I'll see you later?' He ignored her; continuing to look at his phone. 'Sorry,' she said in a low voice. She picked up her jumper from the floor and put it on, and then walked to the bedroom door, turning the gold-coloured brass door handle.

Aimee left Matt's bedroom and went downstairs to the hallway, holding carefully on to the wooden handrail as she came down the stairs. She could smell the home fragrance from the Lavender reed diffuser at the entrance of the hallway, and heard a car parking in the driveway at the front of the house.

Aimee took her coat off the coat rack and put it on, getting ready to leave. As she moved forward to open the oak wood front door to leave, she saw the outline of Matt's mother, Lorraine, on the other side of the front door, through the semi-transparent glass.

Lorraine had put her key in the door lock and was coming into the house; the front door opened and a cold breeze came into the house with her. Lorraine was in her forties, 5 feet 10 in height with black hair and streaks of grey. She was wearing a green quilted jacket and winter scarf and carrying her shopping bag with one hand.

'Aimee!' Lorraine said with a smile and embraced her, 'how are you doing sweetheart, you ok?'

Aimee hesitated, briefly breaking eye contact with Lorraine, 'Yes thanks, I just need to go... bye!'

'Ok!' Lorraine replied as Aimee walked out of the house through the front door. Aimee headed down the driveway and to the pavement of Elbury Road, leaving Lorraine behind with a worried look on her face. She was unsure if Aimee had been crying, or was upset, or just in a hurry to leave. She came into the house and closed the front door behind her, putting down her shopping in the hallway; she put her scarf and keys on the coat rack & shelf, respectively.

Lorraine went upstairs to her son's bedroom. As she walked up the stairs, she thought to herself, '*What has he done now?*' She knocked on his bedroom door and when Matt didn't respond, she entered and walked towards his bed.

As she stood by his bedside looking at him as he sat in the bed, he pretended to ignore her whilst watching the television on his bedroom wall. Lorraine said to her son, 'What did you say to her? You want to keep pushing everyone away don't you? That girl has been through a lot and she doesn't need your....' Lorraine sighed and there was pause as Matt looked at her. '... your negative attitude, your lies and mood swings. What did you say to her Matt? She was upset!'

Lorraine waited as he looked at her in the eye and responded with a sarcastic grin.

'So you're an expert in relationships, are you?' he said viciously.

'Excuse me... Matt what is the problem, is everything ok?' Lorraine asked. There was no response from Matt; he picked up the remote control and turned up the volume of the television. 'Are you still annoyed about what I said this morning? I think you need to watch your attitude,' Lorraine added.

'Sure, whatever,' he replied as he got up from the bed and walked towards the bedroom door shrugging past his mother.

'Where are you going?' Lorraine asked. Matt left the bedroom and went downstairs quickly, and Lorraine followed him, 'Matt don't walk away from me - I am speaking to you!' she said as she stood on the stairs with a hand on the banister. Matt ignored her as he proceeded to put on his jacket. 'When will you be back?' she asked with her arms crossed.

'Don't need to listen to your condescending preaching, thanks' Matt replied, and slammed the front door as he left.

'Matt!!!' Lorraine shouted, then she sighed.

This was the final Academic year of 6th form education for the students at Aston Gate College in Reigate, Surrey, England. They had chosen to study different A Level Subjects, and all of them were attending the same college.

Aimee Larkson was studying *English Literature, Leisure & Tourism, Geography.*

Kat Casado was studying *Drama & Theatre Studies, English Literature, Psychology.*

Matt Morley was studying *English Literature, Economics, Further Maths.*

Leyton Stowell was studying *Media, Leisure & Tourism, Geography.*

Lucy Stearman was studying *Economics,*

Further Maths, Geography.

The next day, Wednesday, in the morning at 7.29am, Aimee was getting ready for college. She looked outside her bedroom window to grey skies. After having a shower, she could hear the chirping of birds outside her window. She was in her towel and took a moment to feel the bedroom carpet under her feet before starting to get dressed. After dressing, she sat on the chair facing her desk, which had a rectangular makeup mirror with LED lights. She gazed in the mirror as she started to apply her makeup. Several small photos of herself and her best friend Kat were stuck all around the sides of the makeup mirror. She picked up her phone and opened WhatsApp to look at the message she sent to Matt last night saying, '*I'm sorry,*' but he had not responded or even seen the message, which worried her as she was certain Matt was very upset because of yesterday afternoon.

Even worse, she worried that he no longer wanted to be with her. Aimee then decided to send another message saying, '*I love u*,' hoping for some kind of response. She kept looking at her WhatsApp messages repeatedly for a few minutes and then she began to worry.

Aimee left her bedroom and went downstairs. Before she reached the bottom of the stairs she could smell food frying. Reaching the bottom stairs she walked into the open plan kitchen and sat at the large rectangular glass breakfast table in the kitchen where her family were already seated.

The house had a large kitchen diner with a marble surface kitchen island, wooden flooring and black bifold doors which opened to the garden. The kitchen had white walls and was very bright as the kitchen ceiling had glass panels allowing natural light to come through.

Aimee's younger brother Tom, who was in his school uniform, sat opposite Aimee at the breakfast table in his own world, just staring at his phone, ignoring his bowl of cereal in front of him. Their stepdad, Jerome, was making a fry up for breakfast.

Jerome was standing opposite the cooker in his navy blue checked pyjamas. Aimee crossed her arms with her elbows on the table. She was hungry, but she could wait a while for Jerome's breakfast; she had always enjoyed his cooking.

'Er how long till breakfast?' she asked, looking at Jerome. Jerome looked back and smiled whilst holding the cooking tongs; Jerome is 6 feet 1 in height and he has a low-cut afro hair with a short beard.

'Unbelievable!' he said, and Aimee smiled at him. Her phone vibrated with a notification; she looked down at it.

'*SORRY about yesterday, were ok*' was the WhatsApp message from Matt which brought a smile to Aimee's face.

Jerome came to the breakfast table moving closer to Aimee and kissed her on the forehead. He put his arm around her, and she put her arms around him as he proceeded to serve breakfast.

He put down three plates on the table: one for himself, one for Aimee and one for Emma - each plate with hash browns, bacon, scrambled eggs, sausages, and baked beans. 'Amazing thanks,' Aimee said, and Jerome then sat down next to Aimee to eat his own breakfast.

'So, what do you want to do for your birthday?' he asked, looking at Aimee.

She looked at him and then shook her head slightly, 'I don't want it to be a big thing!' she responded.

'Aimee are you sure? It's your 18th and oh and I'm sure your mum is plotting something too!' Jerome said. Aimee continued eating breakfast, '...and when are you going to take your theory?' Jerome continued.

Aimee looked at Jerome and replied, 'I haven't booked the theory yet.'

Aimee's mum Emma had made her way downstairs into the kitchen. 'Oh, that smells so good!' she said as she walked into the kitchen. Emma is 41 years old, and she is 6 feet 1 in height. On this day she was dressed in a smart navy double breasted suit with gold detail buttons, a white luxury cotton nylon shirt underneath with tie detail and navy suit trousers. She carried a black luxury Tote bag.

Emma's tucked a stray blonde hair behind her ear – not an easy task with such a short pixie cut. She walked up to Tom, her son, and gave him a hug from behind where he sat and then Emma went to Aimee and gave her daughter a quick kiss on the cheek. Aimee could smell her mum's perfume. Emma proceeded to kiss Jerome on the lips, calling 'Love you!' towards them all as she prepared to leave.

'What about breakfast?' Jerome asked.

'Thanks, sorry I am in a rush – could you put it in the fridge?' Emma said, walking away from the breakfast table to head out into the hallway. She then opened the front door and left for work, closing it softly behind her.

Aimee's younger brother also got up from the breakfast table to leave for school, ignoring his sister and stepdad. As he stood up Aimee said to him inquisitively, 'I see you're spending a lot of time with Charlotte.'

'So?' Tom asked.

'Is she…?' Aimee asked curiously, smiling.

'What is it to you?' her brother responded with a stern look on his face, as he began to blush. He ignored his sister, picked up his bag and walked to the hallway to leave through the front door.

Jerome smiled as he was eating his breakfast. 'Have you seen him with Charlotte?' he asked Aimee.

'I know he's been texting her. I have seen him walking with her outside, so I don't know why he's being so secretive,' she told Jerome and there was a short pause as they continued to eat their breakfast.

'You are going to be 18, I think it's time for your first car and its 2021 sweetheart, so you have plenty of choice of cars to pick from as your present,' Jerome said to Aimee. 'Which car would you want Aimee?' he continued.

Aimee took a deep breath and closed her eyes. 'I definitely have one in mind,' said Aimee, as she picked up her phone and showed Jerome some pictures of the car she quite liked.

He nodded his head and smiled. 'Ok, when you are ready,' he replied. Jerome then put his hand on Aimee's hand. 'Anyway, I am so proud of you to see the growth you have made in life,' he said, there was a pause as he smiled at her. 'I think you are ready to find your own way in this world and well as for Uni only do what makes you proud, what you are really passionate about, and don't listen to anyone else.' As he said this, he held her hand. She nodded in agreement, and by this time they had finished eating breakfast.

Jerome turned to face Aimee as they were both sat next to each other at the breakfast table, 'Listen, before you go, I know it's early, but I got you something.' Jerome proceeded to pull a white gift box, about 7cm by 8cm, out of his pyjama pocket. It was sealed with a black ribbon. He handed it to her.

'Thanks!' she said, and smiled,

'Open it,' said Jerome and Aimee loosened the ribbon, opening the gift box. In it was a silver heart shaped locket which she opened to find a picture of herself on one side and a picture of her biological father who had passed away years ago on the other side. She had her hand over her mouth, taken aback by the gift.

She looked at her stepdad and leaned forward from her chair and hugged him, taking a deep breath in. 'Oh Jerome, thank you' she said, with her voice breaking.

'He would have been so proud of you,' Jerome responded, 'and I am very proud of you too,' he added.

The locket had a chain which Aimee secured around her neck. She wiped a tear from her eye as she got up from her chair, putting her hand on Jerome's shoulder. 'See you later,' she said quietly.

'Take care,' he replied as Aimee left the kitchen and headed to the hallway. Putting her coat on she opened the front door, leaving the house to walk to college. A few minutes later Jerome also left the breakfast table to get changed and ready to go to work.

Aimee was six minutes into her walk to Aston Gate college and it started to rain slightly. She was wearing a black petite hooded crop padded coat, a white jumper, light blue regular jeans, and white trainers.

Her best friend, Kat, had arranged to meet Aimee so they would walk to college together as they usually did. Aimee was walking on the pavement, listening to music through her wireless earphones. The song playing was "Positions" by Ariana Grande. Kat ran up behind Aimee and tapped her on the shoulder and

Aimee turned around and they hugged. Aimee removed her earphones. Kat was 5 feet 8 in height and had brunette chin-length dark hair with pink highlights and a nose piercing. She was wearing a padded hooded longline Parka coat, a dark grey hoodie, dark grey joggers, and white trainers. 'Are you ok?' Kat asked Aimee.

'Yeah' responded Aimee without a smile.

Kat held Aimee's hand looking at her and asked, 'Sure?'

'Yes,' Aimee replied, and Kat put her arm around Aimee's shoulder. The sound of cars passing by on the road was all that could be heard.

'Ok, so I have been thinking about what else we can do next summer when we go to Marbella,' Kat said in excitement. Kat was smiling but, before she continued, she could sense a lack of excitement from Aimee, so she asked her best friend, 'but are you excited Aimz?' looking Aimee in the eye.

'Yea, sure' Aimee responded nodding but

slightly uncomfortable. Kat could sense Aimee was apprehensive about their holiday to Marbella, which they had discussed a few weeks ago but they continued walking.

'Have you told Matt that we're going?' Kat asked as they walked.

Aimee initially hesitated to answer and then she replied, 'I just haven't got round to it.'

'Ok' Kat replied smiling wearily, 'do you want me to do it?'

'No, don't, I will tell him, there is just so much going on with studying and coursework, I will definitely tell Matt about our holiday next summer!' Aimee replied.

'Cool, well it's just me, you and Leyton on holiday so I don't see what the problem is. I am sure Matt will be fine without you for a week, it's going to be great!' Kat responded.

There is no way I can tell him, Aimee thought to herself, wondering how she would tell Matt she is going on holiday next summer without him. Kat and Aimee were still walking to college.

'I spent like an hour talking to Leyton last night, you should have joined us, we had a group call, but you didn't pick up,' Kat said.

'I know, sorry I missed it I was with Matt,' Aimee replied,

'Leyton said that his budget would be £400 for the holiday, and we should definitely check out the Taste of Marbella Food and Market Tour',

'That sounds good.'

'There is diving and snorkelling in Cabo de Gata Natural Park as well.' Kat replied. 'Anyway, we have time before we plan it next year,' Kat added.

'Got a bit emotional this morning, it was Jerome.' Aimee said to Kat, there was a short pause.

'Did he say something to upset you?' Kat asked looking at Aimee.

'No, he's been amazing' Aimee replied, 'he gave me this.' They stopped walking and

Aimee released the locket from her neck and showed it to Kat.

Kat opened it to see the picture of Aimee to the left and the picture of Aimee's dad to the right and she put her hand over her mouth. 'It's beautiful,' she said to Aimee. She stood in front of Aimee, and they hugged.

'Stop you're gonna set me off!' Aimee said to Kat.

Kat held both of Aimee's hands. 'I know you miss him so much, always remember he loved you Aimz,' Kat said with her voice breaking slightly.

Kat wiped a tear from below Aimee's eye with her fingers. Aimee took a deep breath. 'I know,' she replied, they continued to walk and a few minutes later arrived at Aston Gate College. They went past the college gates and at reception scanned their pass to enter, they walked into the college main corridor, Kat going off to attend her Drama class and Aimee to her Geography class.

'See you later!' Kat said to Aimee as they headed to their separate classes.

Later in the afternoon, at 1.54pm, Aimee was sat down in the 6th form common room. The flooring of the common room had dark grey carpeting and there were bright fluorescent lights above in the ceiling and blue double entry doors with a transparent glass panel on either side of the common room. In the common room were dark grey leather sofas, a television on the wall showing the news, and a foosball table. In front of the leather sofas were white round coffee tables with wooden legs. The room had a sound of chatter from the other 6th form students, and you could hear, in the background, the BBC News channel from the television. There was a smell of food from the canteen, and fresh coffee. Aimee's friend Leyton sat opposite to her on the sofa before her next lesson. Leyton is 5 feet 10 in height with short afro hair and a skin fade. 'I told Kat last night that for Marbella we should do at least ten days,' he said to

Aimee.

'That's too much!' Aimee responded and there was an uncomfortable pause. Leyton sat back in the sofa and was smiling,

'What?' Aimee asked curiously. Leyton brought out his mobile phone and showed her a picture on his phone. Aimee got up and moved to sit next to him on the sofa. She leaned closer to him looking at the picture on his phone. 'Is that your car?' Aimee asked, she smiled,

'Yes, I got it just yesterday,' said Leyton,

'Nice, so now that you've passed, you should be driving us around Surrey mate,' Aimee replied,

'You wish!'

'You might even drive us all the way to Spain!'

'Maybe I will,' he responded sarcastically. Leyton looked at Aimee, eye to eye, 'It's nice to see you smiling Aimee, I haven't seen you smile in while.' Aimee flicked her hair backwards and smiled at Leyton.

'Where is Kat, I haven't seen her today?' Leyton asked.

'She has rehearsals for the play,' Aimee replied.

Aimee looked at Leyton maintaining eye contact. 'Is your mum ok?' she asked.

Leyton paused and looked to the floor of the common room; he sat forward with hands clasped together. 'Yes, well she is getting used to going out of the house by herself now, stepping out, going to the shops, she doesn't go far, and she only leaves the house during the day, but even to walk to the corner shop or the post office by herself is a way back to normality,' Leyton continued. 'She still has some nightmares, and she doesn't go out at night ever since she got mugged, but having the confidence to leave the house is a step in the right direction.'

Aimee put her hand behind Leyton's back to comfort him, to show that she cared. 'I'm sorry,' she said.

'It's not your fault.' Leyton replied. They

were interrupted by Matt as he came up behind them walking up to the sofa and once Leyton saw Matt he moved away from Aimee, moving further down the sofa. Aimee quickly withdrew her hand from Leyton's back and Leyton got up to leave for his next lesson. 'Hi Matt,' he said briefly. 'See you soon,' he said to Aimee, avoiding any eye contact with Matt. Matt watched Leyton leave the common room.

Matt put his hands on Aimee's shoulders and stood behind her in the common room, he leaned down to her ear. 'What was that about?' he asked.

'Nothing'

'Didn't look like nothing.'

'I mean, it's about his mum,' Aimee replied. Aimee put her hand behind her neck, 'Look I have to go,' Aimee said to Matt, they kissed briefly.

'Hey, look at me!' Matt said to Aimee, putting his hand on her chin and drawing her chin towards him, 'is there something you want to tell me or ask me?' he added.

In that moment Aimee remembered about the holiday to Marbella, she thought *'maybe this is the moment to tell him'* but she hesitated. 'No,' she responded, quietly.

'Come and stay with me tonight?' asked Matt, there was a pause.

'Maybe tomorrow,' Aimee replied, 'I want to finish my coursework and some revision tonight.' They kissed. Matt sat down on the sofa in the common room and Aimee got up and went to her next lesson.

That evening Leyton was at Aimee's house, he arrived at 49 Faircroft Road in Reigate, Surrey, around 7.02pm. He was in her bedroom as they both planned to exchange notes and revise Geography A Level together.

They sat opposite to each other on the carpeted floor of her bedroom, Aimee's room had a pleasant fragrance of strawberry scented oil from the fragrance plug-in diffusers in her room. In her bedroom were two bedside tables with table lamps on each, a double bed, a built-in floor to ceiling wardrobe, chest of drawers, a desk with chair and a cream upholstered rocking chair. Leyton felt at ease and relaxed in her bedroom. He was wearing a navy-blue oversized graffiti print hoodie, navy blue tracksuit, and black socks. Aimee was wearing a grey hoodie and grey joggers. 'I want to go to either Manchester or Warwick University, that would be my first choice,' Aimee said to Leyton, 'and you?' she asked Leyton.

'Not sure about where I want to go for Uni, will need to think about it but I have been through the prospectus for South Bank and Middlesex Unis,' he said.

'Regardless of what I study, what I am like really passionate about is teaching English abroad to children, just watching them engaged and smiling,' Aimee said.

'You can do it Aimee, you'd be great!' Leyton responded and smiled.

'By the way there is a Ministry of Sound club near London South Bank Uni in

Elephant and Castle, you can party at night and do lectures in the day, you would love it, like that would be your life!' they both smiled, there was a pause, he leaned forward facing Aimee.

'Basically, our summer holiday will be the last time all of us will be together before we start Uni, me you and Kat,' he said.

'You know she will get us in a lot of trouble in Marbella?'

'Guaranteed, that's the fun of it,' Leyton got up from the carpeted floor of Aimee's bedroom, he noticed the gift box on her desk, he walked to the desk. 'Can I see it?' he asked, Aimee nodded. He stood in front of the desk and opened the box to see the locket Aimee received earlier in the day and looked inside to see the picture of Aimee and her dad. He put the locket back in the gift box, there was a pause, he looked over to her. 'Do you still remember him? ...... sorry I shouldn't ask,' said Leyton. He was referring to Aimee's dad who passed away years ago.

'Yes,' Aimee replied, 'especially when I am

in the garden or if I go to the park, because we spent so much time there.' There were a few seconds of silence as she reflected and before her emotions could get the better of her, she cleared her throat and changed the topic of conversation. 'Anyway tell me about your driving test - how did you pass?' she asked.

Leyton laughed. 'What do you mean how did I pass?' he responded. 'I told you take the test around 11am, its quieter, there are less cars on the road but also I did the test without my instructor, less stressful!' he added.

A few minutes later the conversation continued. 'Can I ask, do you feel you are in a good place with your stepdad, with Jerome?' Leyton asked.

'He's great, just great, he's been really supportive, and he cares,' Aimee replied.

'Good for you,' said Leyton, there was a pause.

Aimee took out her phone and scrolled through her previous photos, stopping at an older picture of herself with Kat. She showed it to Leyton on her phone, Leyton leaned closer to Aimee and they both laughed at a picture of Kat's hair soaked in paint, as they laughed together Leyton then put his hand on Aimee's knee. Aimee looked at his hand and, still smiling, moved her knee away. She cleared her throat as she said to Leyton, 'Ok so for A-level Geography, we have physical geography and human geography, erm under physical geography there is water and carbon cycles, here are my notes on water cycles,' she showed her notepad with colour highlighted notes to Leyton.

'And I have some practice questions,' Leyton responded, handing over a printout of sample questions to Aimee, 'They are fr....' before Leyton could finish speaking, they could hear Aimee's parents arguing loudly downstairs.

Aimee sighed and then closed her eyes. 'Sorry about that,' she said.

'It's ok, don't worry about it.' Leyton responded whilst sat down next to Aimee.

'It's not ok,' Aimee got up and in frustration closed shut the door of her bedroom, whilst standing she leaned with her back against the door, put both hands on her head and pulled them back over her hair taking a deep breath, 'they always pick the worst moments to argue even in public!' Aimee said to Leyton, she then sat down on her bed with her legs crossed.

'Does it make you uncomfortable when they are fighting?' Leyton asked.

'It's not even... I mean they just have a go at each other over the smallest things, my mum makes it worse, she will never lose an argument.' Aimee exclaimed and there was a pause. Leyton got up and sat on Aimee's bed next to her.

'And your parents?' Aimee asked looking at Leyton.

'I have never heard them fight or argue or raise their voice at each other.'

'You're lucky!'

'Anyway, Kat and I are excited for our break to Marbella, let us know what you want to do as well when we go,' there was a pause then Leyton added, 'By the way my sister is getting married', immediately Aimee clapped and put her hands up in excitement, she was smiling.

'It would be good for you to come to the wedding in June,' said Leyton.

'Of course,!!' Aimee replied.

'She still asks about you all the time, she's obsessed with you: "When am I going to see Aimee?" he said with a sarcastic voice imitating his sister, "When is she coming over?" Aimee was smiling.

'Sorry I haven't been to yours in a while,' Aimee said, 'will say hi to Karis next time I see her,' she added.

Another twenty-eight minutes had passed in which Aimee and Leyton continued to revise Geography A-Level. Leyton put down his AQA textbook and looked over to Aimee. She noticed he was looking at her. 'What?' she asked. Leyton hesitated to answer, then he shook his head. Aimee put her hand on Leyton's shoulder, 'Tell me!'

she said.

'Do you think about the future with Matt?' Leyton asked and there was a long pause.

'Leyton why would you ask me that?' Aimee said.

'Sorry, I mean are you happy with him?'

Aimee closed her mouth biting the bottom of her inner lip, she had a slightly confused look on her face. 'That's a strange question to ask me, where is that coming from?' she asked.

Before Leyton could respond Aimee added, 'I am happy, and I trust him and I can talk to him about anything,' she cleared her throat and crossed her arms, sitting up in the bed with her back against the headboard. Leyton nodded his head slowly and continued reading; they finished revising and making notes, Leyton left the Larkson house two hours later, heading home around 10.05pm.

Half an hour later Aimee changed into her pyjamas and brushed her teeth, ready for bed. There was a knock on her bedroom door. 'Come in,' she said. Aimee's stepdad, Jerome, came in to the bedroom with a cup of tea and digestive biscuits on a plate. He placed the cup of tea and small plate on her bedside table. Aimee sat up in bed and took in the smell of the Lemon & Ginger tea. Jerome sat on the bedside, he sighed. 'I know you've heard me and your mum arguing and I'm sorry if it has upset you.'

'Do you enjoy winding her up?' Aimee asked.

'No, it's just when we disagree well sometimes it gets emotional,' Jerome replied.

'Every time!'

'What?'

'Every time you disagree it gets emotional!' said Aimee, there was a pause.

'Leyton was here for a while, you two had a lot to talk about?' he asked. Aimee nodded but didn't say anything, she sipped her tea.

'His mum is doing better?' Jerome asked.

'Yes, she is. I should go and see her soon,

see how she's doing,' Aimee replied.

'Is everything ok with you? It's just in recent days you have been quieter than usual,' he said.

'Yes, I'm good,' Aimee replied.

'And you and Matt?' Jerome asked, Aimee took a deep breath and nodded.

'I get the sense you are starting to think about Matt longer term. You have been together nearly three years now,' said Jerome. 'Well Matt is smart and his heart seems to be in the right place,' he added. Jerome got up from Aimee's bedside and walked towards her bedroom door. 'If you ever want to talk just let me know,' he added.

As Jerome turned the bedroom door handle to leave, Aimee said to him, 'Thanks!' holding up the cup of tea. 'Sometimes I feel like we are drifting apart, like our values are different.' Aimee said to Jerome.

'You mean Matt?' Jerome asked.

'Yes, he's changing, becoming more

popular than I am, everyone likes him, sometimes I get jealous of that.' said Aimee. 'I think what if he gets....... bored of me, just stops caring?' she added.

'Aimee don't think like that and don't compare yourself to him,' Jerome replied looking at Aimee.

'One day he just leaves and then I'm alone,' she said.

'If he stays, leaves, all that matters is we love you. I love you, just be yourself,' Jerome said smiling, he opened the bedroom door and whilst closing it said to Aimee, 'Goodnight.'

A few minutes later Aimee went downstairs to the kitchen to get a glass of water, the kitchen lights were dimly lit. She met her mum in the kitchen; Emma was sat on a bar stool in front of the kitchen island, her arms folded with a wine glass and bottle of wine next to her. Aimee walked to the fridge she poured a glass of water from the water dispenser and sat at the kitchen island opposite her mum, there was a pause.

Emma looked at her daughter. 'I know what you're thinking,' she said to Aimee, 'Listen I'm always going to stand my ground with him,' she added.

'I didn't say you shouldn't mum.'

Emma stretched out her hands forward on the marble surface of the kitchen island. 'If it makes you uncomfortable, sorry!' Emma said.

'But you never try to find a compromise, that's the problem, and you never give him a chance to speak his mind mum.' Emma smiled briefly, then drank from the wine glass.

'Anyway, I thought you were revising so you shouldn't have heard any of that,' she said to Aimee.

'It gets quite intense when you're arguing,' Aimee replied raising her voice in frustration.

Emma put down her wine glass and got up from the bar stool, moved closer to her daughter, standing next to her. Taking her by the hand, she said to Aimee, 'Listen, relationships are not about nodding your head all the time, even with your dad bless his soul - we had our moments, but you were younger then. Are you telling me you don't argue with Matt? You think your lives will be like that forever?'

'No, we do argue sometimes but we don't make it an issue, I just avoid saying something and he says nothing too, there is no need for confrontation,' Aimee said to her mum.

'That's even worse, sweetheart, because it leads to resentment and resentment will build up over time,' Emma replied.

Aimee looked away from her mum and crossed her arms whilst sat on the bar stool, 'and when it all comes out you will say and do things you never expected Aimee. If you are not happy about something tell him, speak your mind, don't sweep anything under the carpet and hope it will go away,' Emma added. 'Are you worried about how he might react?' Emma asked.

'No,' Aimee replied looking down at the kitchen island worktop.

'Look at me,' Emma said to Aimee softly, putting her hand on her daughter's shoulder, there was a moment of silence as they just looked at each other.

Aimee sighed, 'Yes I am worried cause he gets agitated or just stops talking if I do something wrong, and that makes me feel uncomfortable,' Aimee said.

Emma replied, 'Aimee you have to speak your mind always and express how you feel, if something bothers you say it.'

'Well, I am not happy with people thinking Matt and I are not ok mum, that's what annoys me,' said Aimee. Emma took a deep breath in.

'Well, he better be on his best behaviour otherwise he's got me to deal with,' Emma said, she hugged her daughter. 'It's not all butterflies and kisses sweetheart,' Emma added.

Emma left the kitchen but as she got to the

bottom of the staircase, Aimee shouted to her from the kitchen. 'Mum, by the way Karis is getting married and you're invited!'

'Leyton's sister? How nice, where and when?' Emma asked, with one foot on the bottom of the stairs.

'Moreton In Marsh, in June.'

'A wedding in the Cotswolds, very nice, I will text her, I'm going to bed, goodnight,' said Emma whilst walking up the stairs.

The next day was Thursday, both Leyton and Aimee were at college. They attended their geography lesson at 10am and sat next to each other. The sun started to shine through the windows of Aston Gate college's building, the classroom had brilliant white walls with square recessed ceiling lighting, navy blue carpeted flooring, a large world map on the wall, blue cushioned chairs and white desks.

Aimee looked at Leyton and smiled, he

smiled back, they were in a classroom of fifteen students including themselves. Leyton leaned towards Aimee, 'You look great,' he said, 'I bought something you might be interested in. Do you want to come to mine tonight? We can watch it!' he added.

'Show me,' Aimee asked, they both were facing forward pretending to focus on the whiteboard. Leyton took out his phone and opened the Gallery app, he showed Aimee a picture of the *N-Dubz* concert DVD he bought.

'Live at the O2,' he whispered and put his phone away.

A minute later Aimee said to Leyton, 'I would love to see it, not sure about tonight but we should fix a date.' Leyton nodded, there was a pause, 'But on one condition,' said Aimee, she put her hand on his arm, 'you have to show me how to use your mixing deck, the one you got for your birthday,' she added.

'It's not for amateurs Aimee it cost like over five grand,' he replied.

'So, teach me!'

'Hmm!' said Leyton, there was a pause, he put forward his hand by his side and under the desk, then said, 'deal!' Aimee shook Leyton's hand, both were smiling, the geography lesson continued.

It was now lunchtime and Matt was sat in the 6th form common room. He was wearing a white t-shirt with a navy-blue jacket over it and dark grey skinny jeans, white trainers. Lucy Stearman another 6th former walked up behind him and tapped him on the shoulder. As Matt was sat down, she proceeded to sit next to him on the sofa, Lucy was 5 feet 10 in height with long brunette hair and blonde highlights. She was wearing a white crop top with an open blue denim jacket over it, and blue denim ripped jeans, black suede block heel Chelsea boots. 'Ok,' she said smiling, 'so your dad is a planning some kind of fitness boot camp and endurance run with my dad? A 10k run?' she asked Matt.

Looking confused, Matt sighed, 'I don't

know, I don't talk to him Lucy, he can do whatever.' he sat back and spread out his arms on the common room sofa, looking away from Lucy.

'You don't talk to him at all?' Lucy asked, there was a pause.

'Both of them together, that's a disaster!' Matt added shaking his head.

'I know,' Lucy replied smiling, she added, 'they are having a midlife crisis!'

Matt laughed. 'Basically!' he said in response.

'How are you finding Economics and Further Maths?' Lucy asked, with her finger she flicked her hair back, tilted her face sideways looking at Matt.

Matt replied, 'Economics is great its Further Maths that's a little difficult,' he sighed.

'Why?'

'It's the statistics I am trying to get my head around.'

'Don't worry about it!' Lucy put her left

hand on Matt's right knee. 'Come over I can help you understand it better, show you how I approach statistics,' she added.

Matt nodded his head, 'Ok!' he said.

'I'm free tonight if that works for you or whenever you want just let me know,' said Lucy, 'see you later,' she said to Matt. Lucy touched Matt's shoulder as she got up to leave the common room, she headed to the doors of the common room carrying her bag, as Lucy walked away Matt looked at her and smirked.

A few hours later it was 4.10pm, Aimee had finished her lessons for the day, she was ready to leave Aston Gate College and Matt was waiting for her outside the gates. The sound of traffic with cars and vans passing by outside the college as Matt stood on the roadside was penetrating the silence. When Aimee came out to the front gate of the college, Matt put his arms around her and they walked together. As they were walking Matt said, 'I need to speak to you about something, I've been thinking and I want us to be in the same

Uni, Aimee, so we can see each other next year.' Aimee hesitated to respond, *'but I want to go with Kat'* she thought to herself.

'What, is that not what you want?' Matt asked.

Aimee replied cautiously 'No I just thought I might want to go to a different Uni, or I might want to go with Kat, I haven't made up my mind,' she put her hand around his back. 'It all depends on what I want to study,' Aimee added, carefully.

'Kat?' Matt asked Aimee, his face lowered he looked away from Aimee, Aimee tried to put her arms around his waist hoping Matt would be at ease, more relaxed.

'This is a great chance for us to experience Uni life together and you said you wanted us to have new experiences,' Matt added looking at Aimee.

Aimee bit the inside of her bottom lip, they stopped on the pavement, 'I will still see you of course,' Aimee said nervously.

He then held her by the shoulder,

putting his hands on both her shoulders, 'Regardless of what degree we study, you need me around, it's always been us.' Matt said. 'Like, I know you better than Kat or anyone else. They won't have the time for you, to support you,' Matt added. He held her face with the palm of his hands, and said, 'anyway I don't want Uni to be an issue for us,' he said, doubt was expressed on Aimee's face as they continued to walk home.

That evening Matt was in his bedroom, he picked up his phone and called Aimee. As he was talking to Aimee, Matt left his bedroom to go downstairs, into the kitchen for a glass of water. His mother, Lorraine, was in the kitchen cooking. Matt poured water from the water filter into the glass he was holding. He then sat on the chair opposite the kitchen island, in the middle of the large kitchen.

Matt spoke into his phone. 'Look I know we will be studying different degrees but we should both apply to the same

Universities'. Matt could sense Aimee's hesitation on the other end. He pressed on. '...but you know, whatever Uni you choose to go to, you will do great, and I will support you. If we don't go to the same Uni, then at least in the same city so we can see each other regularly, what do you think?'

Aimee's quiet response at the other end of the phone was a simple, 'OK.'

Matt smiled. 'Good.... I must go, will speak to you later'.

Aimee replied with a 'Love you, bye'.

Lorraine overheard the conversation as she was preparing dinner in the kitchen, Matt ended the call.

Lorraine said to her son, 'Don't you think she should choose what she wants to do, where she wants to go?'

'Who said she can't choose?'

'Oh, so you are giving her a choice then?'

'She has a choice. I am not forcing her to

do anything.'

Lorraine shook her head, she opened the oven and put in a tray of potatoes. She faced her son and said, 'Hmm, so it is either she goes to a University near you, or she goes to the same University as you?' Matt shook his head and scoffed as Lorraine said this. 'I see what you are doing,' Lorraine added,

'Oh, and what's that then?' Matt asked.

'You will make her feel bad about it, with your emotional blackmail, then get her to agree with you. I see right through you,' Lorraine picked up her glass of red wine and took a sip, Matt got up from the chair.

'Whatever!' he said.

'Just like your father, he used to do that all the time, he would say all the good things you wanted to hear, just to have his way all the time!'

'Don't compare me to him!' Matt raised his voice and kicked the kitchen chair in annoyance; he left the kitchen and went back upstairs to his bedroom.

It was Sunday afternoon, 12.25pm, the day of Aimee's 18th birthday. Emma had earlier presented a birthday cake and had given Aimee her birthday gift, Kat had called hours earlier to wish happy birthday to her best friend and Aimee's grandmother, June, had called earlier also. Jerome had booked an adventure day as a surprise for Aimee's birthday; he and Aimee were going to the adventure day which included activities, crossbow shooting, indoor assault rifle, and archery.

Emma, Jerome, and Aimee were standing in the hallway, Jerome put his coat on, covering his jumper. He was also wearing navy blue chino trousers and shoes. Aimee was wearing a denim jacket over a black t-shirt with black skinny jeans and trainers. Jerome moved towards Emma and kissed her on the lips. 'Have fun,' Emma said closing the front door behind them. Jerome and Aimee walked to the driveway, Jerome pushed the door open button on the key fob to unlock the car doors while Aimee pulled the handle of the car front door on the passenger side and stepped into the white Renault Kadjar. She adjusted herself in the car seat and put her seatbelt on; Jerome was sat in the driver's seat; he selected navigation on the car's infotainment system and put in the postcode of their destination. The satellite navigation showed the journey time and drive to Romford, Greater London was 56 minutes from their location, Jerome pushed the start/stop button of the car which turned the engine on and started to drive, exiting the driveway carefully.

For a few minutes whilst driving and after leaving the house there was no conversation in the car, Aimee and Jerome did not speak, it was just the sound of the radio from the car's built-in speakers, playing in the background was "Steal My Girl" by One Direction, the car was now heading onto the M25.

Aimee was smiling as she looked outside the car window. 'What?' Jerome asked looking at her briefly as he noticed her smile.

'I'm just remembering last year,' Aimee replied as she looked over to him. 'I had a really good time,' she said and he nodded.

'Well happy birthday, superstar!' Jerome replied. 'Last year was great, up at the O2,' he added whilst looking ahead at the motorway. 'You did really well when you consider your fear of heights,' Jerome added.

'Excuse me, I don't have a fear of heights, it was pretty high up!' Aimee replied.

Jerome laughed. 'You wanted to go back halfway through the climb!'

'But I finished, didn't I?' she said.

Jerome replied, 'I remember there was Emma in front of you, I was behind you and Tom behind me, and you stopped and were like, "I think I want to go back down." Aimee said nothing.

Twelve minutes into the drive, on the motorway, Jerome looked at Aimee and asked, 'Everything ok with you and Matt?'

Her face was expressionless as she looked out the window crossing her arms.

'We're ok!' Aimee replied, there was a short pause.

'Has he called you today?' Jerome asked, she shook her head letting Jerome know Matt hadn't called her to wish her a happy birthday.

Jerome turned down the volume of the car speakers and said, 'Aimee there is something I have wanted to tell you, this isn't just about relationships but in life you are going to be in situations where people will want you to do something for them, which you do not want to do or agree with. You might feel pressured or feel guilty for saying no, but you have to think about what is best for you. They might make you feel like you are the worst person in the world for not doing what they wanted but you have to think of yourself!' Aimee was quiet but she nodded that she had heard and taken in all that Jerome had said.

A minute later Jerome asked Aimee, 'Have

you seen him lose his temper before?' referring to Matt.

Aimee sighed, 'I don't want to talk about this,' she said and she shook her head.

'Aimee sweetheart if he has a temper now, at this age, and doesn't address it, it will not go away and before anything else, this is how you define character,' said Jerome. Aimee cleared her throat and looked straight ahead at the car windscreen; Jerome continued to focus on his driving.

'The last person I hurt, I am reminded every day of what I did to them in the past because of my temper,' he added.

Aimee turned and looked at him, 'But what about your temper now?' she asked.

Jerome looked straight ahead, 'I know it's intense when we argue but your mum is even more head strong than I am Aimee, my temper is fine,' he replied.

A few minutes later Jerome asked Aimee, 'So do you feel any different now you're

18?'

'Yes,' Aimee replied, she added, 'I am now certain that my self-actualisation is helping people, particularly teaching. I was saying to Leyton a few days ago that I would love to teach English overseas to children,' Jerome smiled nodding his head in agreement.

Later, after driving for almost an hour, when they were getting closer to the venue that held the activity day, Jerome and Aimee decided to get something to eat. Jerome drove into the drive-through at McDonalds in Romford. As Jerome drove the car in, 'Hi what is your order?' was the question and voice from the intercom.

'Erm double cheeseburger and an Apple Pie,' replied Jerome leaning his head out of the rolled down car window, he then looked at Aimee, she nodded, 'spot on!' she said.

'Anything else?' asked the voice from the intercom.

Jerome replied, 'For me a triple cheeseburger and nuggets, one strawberry milkshake to share thanks.' He drove forwards and within minutes they picked up their order from the drive-through, Jerome then drove their car to the venue.

They arrived at the activity day venue, the car was parked at the customers parking area, Aimee and Jerome stayed in the car for a few more minutes to finish their takeaway food.

They got out of the car and went to the reception of the venue to sign in, the host of the activity day waited eleven more minutes for other visitors booked in the same session to arrive. The host was wearing a black t-shirt and black jeans and he had a bald head. Jerome and Aimee were standing next to the host, Jerome standing with his arms crossed. 'Right follow me! I will take you to the first activity' the host said, shouting across the room, there were six other people that joined Jerome and Aimee, he led them all down a corridor and to the indoor shooting range. When they got to the entrance of the indoor shooting range, there was a row of rectangular tables covered with a black cloth, a grey plastic chair behind each table, the tables had protective screens between them, each table had on it a semi-automatic rifle with scope, ear protection, safety goggles for the eyes and a magazine with 25 rounds. Jerome and Aimee took a seat, Jerome's table was next to Aimee's, for the first activity, the indoor assault rifle shooting, the rifle instructor went through the safety briefing with everyone.

When the session started, Aimee put on her safety wear. She held the mounted rifle which was tethered to the desk and looked down the view scope, cautiously controlling her breathing as she held the rifle steady. Focussing on her view through the rifle scope, she aimed at her target which was a shooting target chart with circles. She pulled back the trigger, releasing the bullets, as she sat back, she could smell a burning smell from the release of the bullets, she turned to her side and looked to Jerome, he looked at her and they both smiled, Jerome then gestured giving her the thumbs up.

When the session was finished, they walked to the end of the shooting range, standing in front of their target charts. Aimee looked at her chart, the bullets had hit the black inner circles and the red inner circles, she was pleased, Jerome was surprised as most of his shots had hit the outer circles.

They moved on to the next session; crossbow shooting. Jerome and Aimee had the highest score within the group. The host gave them an award for having the most accurate shots in the group.

Hours later, Aimee and Jerome came out of the venue laughing, in high spirits. As they were walking back to the car, Aimee approaching the front passenger door, her phone rang. Aimee answered the call which was from Leyton, who had called to wish her Happy Birthday and even sang to her, making Aimee smile. Jerome was already sat in the car, in the driver's seat, Aimee got into the car sitting in the front passenger seat. 'Thank you for today,' Aimee said to Jerome looking at him beaming with a huge smile.

'My pleasure, I had a great time!' Jerome replied. Jerome then drove them back home to Reigate, Surrey.

It was the following weekend on a Saturday in the evening, 7.52pm. That evening, Matt and Aimee were preparing to attend the birthday party of their fellow 6th former, Lewis. The birthday party was a house party near Reigate Heath in Surrey. Matt was in Aimee's bedroom watching her as she got ready for the part. He sat in the cream upholstered rocking chair opposite her bed. The bedroom was a warm cosy environment, the walls painted white, her double bed neatly arranged with emerald green and gold print cushions over the bed pillows; the bedside lamps, which were on, a soft rug at the foot of the bed between the bed and rocking chair.

Aimee had put on her outfit that she had chosen for the party, a perfectly fitting navy-blue dress with a plunge neckline and with a thigh split. She picked up her perfume from the bedside table and sprayed it on her neck, as she faced the standing mirror she smiled slightly, turning to the side also as she looked to the mirror, Matt was looking at his phone as he sat down. He looked up at Aimee, he then asked, 'Why are you wearing that it's a bit revealing don't you think?' there was an uncomfortable pause and Aimee had a confused look on her face. 'I mean it might get quite cold when we are outside,' he added, 'so maybe you want to try something else?'

'You don't think I look good in it? I spent forty pounds on this dress!' Aimee replied, clearly irritated.

'Don't raise your voice at me,' Matt snapped and Aimee sighed, 'Whatever, just be quick' he added.

Aimee took off the Navy Blue Dress and

lay It on her bed. 'I should wear what I like,' she said to herself muttering, she was in her bra and underwear.

'What?' Matt responded, 'Did you say something?' he added as he was looking at his phone.

'Nothing,' Aimee replied, she tried to look for another outfit from her wardrobe but, after five minutes could not find an outfit, she liked. 'I like that one,' she said to Matt pointing to the navy-blue dress on the bed.

'I know but you can do better; something classier, that dress is a bit much!' said Matt. Aimee had a blank expression on her face, she walked forward and looked Matt in the eye,

'So, you don't want me to go out?' she asked.

'Course I want you to come, you should be there with me, stop making this an issue!' said Matt. Aimee stood in front of him with her arms folded as he sat on the chair.

She said, 'I don't understand, you have a problem when I don't dress up or you say it is not attractive enough, and now you're saying what I am wearing is too revealing.'

Matt got up and faced her, saying to Aimee with a calm voice, 'You don't want to embarrass yourself with people making comments, lets hurry up.' He put his hands on Aimee's shoulders, 'Let's go!' he added.

'No let's talk about this now!' Aimee said in frustration, Matt shook his head.

'I can leave you here, go by myself to the party then, if you are going to make a fuss,' he said. Aimee sighed but did not respond to Matt, she investigated the wardrobe again put on her black skinny jeans and a short navy blue and white dotted floral blouse. As Aimee was getting changed, Matt looked at his phone, he sent a WhatsApp message to Lucy: *Will u be there?* and was awaiting a response from her, hoping to see her at Lewis's birthday party. He left Aimee's bedroom and went downstairs.

Matt was wearing a black bomber jacket with a cream turtleneck jumper underneath, navy-blue skinny jeans and black suede shoes. He turned to the mirror in the hallway to look at himself and adjust his hair. As he was adjusting his hair, he thought to himself *Lucy will be there tonight*.

Aimee left her bedroom and came downstairs to the hallway. She walked to the front door; Jerome was sat in the living room watching television and shouted, 'Have a good evening both of you!'

'You take care of her!' Emma said to Matt standing in the hallway.

'I will,' he replied, smiling. Aimee took her coat off the coat rack, opened the front door and Matt put his hand behind her back. Their walk from Aimee's house to the house party in Reigate Heath took about twenty minutes; they held hands and walked together.

They had been walking for ten minutes and as they were walking Matt said to Aimee, 'Listen, in a few days' time I am going to see my dad in Bath, it may be a little awkward because *she* is going to be there.'

'She?' Aimee asked.

'His new girlfriend, he wants me to make an effort to meet her.' Matt replied, There was a pause before he sighed, 'She is like 20 years younger than him!' Matt added.

'Sorry to hear that, how old is she?' Aimee asked.

'She's 24.'

'Wow!' Aimee said surprised.

'It's literally a car crash!' Matt added and there was another pause. 'Sorry,' Matt said.

'That's ok' Aimee responded, she then cleared her throat, 'just make the effort to get on with both of them,' she added.

They continued walking and had now been walking for 19 minutes; they were close to the house party, it was dark in the evening so Matt brought out his phone and turned on the torch on his phone to see the footpath clearly. They approached the electric black wooden front gate of the house in Reigate Heath, and pushed the button on the intercom, you could hear the music coming from the house, it was "Sandstorm" by Darude. The front gate opened slowly revealing the driveway, Aimee held Matt back and took him by the hand, she walked to the side of the front gate taking Matt with her. 'Sorry there was something I really wanted to talk to you about,' Aimee said to Matt.

'Can this wait?' he asked looking at the gate, 'come on!' Matt said. He didn't stop to find out what Aimee wanted to talk about.

They walked through the driveway of the house. As they approached the front door of the house the security light came on as it detected their motion. Aimee had a worried look on her face, she insisted to let Matt know what was on her mind. Aimee pulled on Matt's arm and looked at him. 'Look, next weekend I want to go and see my nan, just spend the weekend with her. I haven't seen her in a while Matt.' she said. They were now both stood at the front door of the house and Matt sighed. 'Well I was thinking maybe we do something special next weekend, you should have told me earlier,' Matt responded.

'Ok, well I'm sorry I didn't tell you earlier!' Aimee said raising her voice. Matt put his hand on Aimee's shoulder and said, 'Look let's just enjoy Lewis's party tonight. Ok we will talk about it another time.'

'That's his way of saying no' she thought to herself, disappointed.

'And don't be moody tonight, I want to have fun!' Matt said to Aimee.

Lewis opened the front door, and Matt and Aimee were let into the house party. The house was a large 4-bedroom detached newly built home with a front garage. Matt received a firm embrace from his best friend Lewis. 'Come right through lad!' Lewis shouted, with a beer in hand; both of them leaving Aimee standing alone at the front door. It was Lewis's 18th birthday; Matt and Lewis both walked into the house party through the hallway.

'Is Lucy here?' Matt asked Lewis leaning to

Lewis's ear as he put his arm around him.

'No she's not coming mate,' Lewis replied. There were over 60 people at the party in different areas of the house, some were in the large living room, some in the dining room and kitchen, some in the hallway, the bedrooms and some in the front and rear gardens. Inside the house there was engineered Rustic Oak wood flooring, which was brushed & lacquered throughout the house, bright white walls with white ceilings, gold detail on every door handle and door hinge. In the L-shaped hallway to the left was an open plan kitchen with a central island, a dining table and access to the rear garden via bi-folding doors. To the right of the hallway a living room with a modern, circular gold chandelier hanging from the ceiling, a large sofa, and some chairs. The living room also had large bi-folding doors leading to the front garden; downstairs was the wine cellar, cinema room and guest WC, upstairs the bedrooms, bathroom, and a huge walk-in wardrobe.

"Head & Heart" by Joel Corry featuring MNEK was playing, blasting through the indoor speakers. Matt was soon in high spirits - laughing and joking with his friends – and an hour had passed at the party and Matt was not interested in Aimee or even talking to her. Aimee looked around the house and spoke to a few sixth formers in the living room, eventually deciding to go to the rear garden. As she entered the large garden she saw wooden decking at the entrance with built in floor lights at each corner. Further into the garden, rattan furniture, a barbeque grill, outdoor sofa, covered jacuzzi, a 3-seater garden swing and stereo speakers were carefully positioned. She looked around at everyone in the garden and saw Leyton talking to someone, he was towards the back of the garden.

Aimee intended to go and speak to Leyton but wanted to check on Matt first. She approached Matt who was towards the right side of the rear garden talking to friends. Aimee noticed he had been drinking as he was holding a beer in his hand. She tapped on his shoulder and looked at him, 'Matt look at me, are you ok? Please no more drinking!'

He shrugged his shoulder, 'Yes I'm fine what do you want?' before Aimee could respond, Lewis jumped on Matt's back and proceeded to put ice cubes at his back through the neck of his top.

Aimee moved back as Matt shouted, 'It's cold!' Lewis and others laughed and Aimee shook her head.

'Guys that is not funny!' she said as Matt eventually removed the ice cubes from his clothing.

'You bastards!' he said. Matt put his arm around Lewis and put him in a headlock eventually releasing him. At this moment in the party, the chorus of "21 Seconds" by So Solid Crew was playing loudly through the stereo speakers in the garden. Lewis and Matt started to jump up and down together singing loudly. Aimee walked to the back of the garden. She approached Leyton, at which time Leyton was talking to a classmate, another 6th former named Danielle. Danielle saw Aimee approaching and moved forward to hug Aimee, 'Hello you!' Danielle said to Aimee. Aimee smiled in return; Leyton and Aimee sat on the garden rattan chairs and Danielle remained standing. Danielle leaned down towards Leyton and put her hand on his shoulder, 'I will speak to you in a bit,' she said to Leyton and then she left Aimee and Leyton to talk together.

'I haven't seen you in while, hope you are doing well,' Aimee said, and Leyton nodded with a slight smile. Leyton and Aimee sat opposite each other, 'I was thinking maybe we can go see a film next week, or we finally watch the "N-Dubz" dvd you have?' Aimee smiled; she leaned forward closer to him.

Leyton looked over to Matt who was standing about eight meters away from them. 'Maybe you should tell him to take it easy!' Leyton said to Aimee, looking across the garden at Matt. Aimee turned her head towards Matt's direction and they both watched as Matt started losing his balance and stumbling. Aimee got up from the rattan chair to walk towards Matt, suddenly Leyton grabbed her wrist pulling her back. 'Don't!' he said shaking his head, there was a pause as they looked at each other. Leyton sighed, 'You're wasting your time, he is just gonna get aggressive with you Aimee,' he said sadly.

'That's my problem not yours,' she said to Leyton; he lowered his head in disappointment. 'Let go of me please,' Aimee said, and Leyton released his grip on her wrist.

'You know what, do what you like, Aimee,' he said to her and stood up, facing her. Before Aimee turned away, Leyton asked her, 'Have you told him that you would love to teach English abroad to children in the future? No, because he doesn't care about your future. Does he ask you how you are feeling on every anniversary of your dad passing away? No, because he doesn't care. Have you told him about our holiday to Marbella with Kat next summer? No because you're scared of him, if you confront him now that he's had too much to drink, he will push you away. Yes, because he's not even aware you're still here!' Leyton stepped back and took a deep breath. Aimee's heart sunk. She felt humiliated by Leyton's words - coming from a friend it was painful and she felt heat come over her head and chest. She was angry and she wanted to throw her drink at Leyton, and she was hurt. Instead, she picked up her clutch bag and left the garden. She walked past Matt who didn't even notice her, opened the rear garden doors to get inside the house into the kitchen/dining room.

Aimee wanted to be alone, when she got back inside the house, she went to the downstairs toilet finding it occupied, so she went to the bathroom upstairs, which was vacant, and locked the door. Aimee sat down on the bathroom floor with her back to the bathroom door and sobbed. Leyton was still in the garden with his head down and eyes closed regretting what he said to Aimee. *Why did you do that,* Leyton thought to himself. He left the garden and looked around the house party for Aimee, hoping she hadn't left. He asked another sixth former at the party, 'Have you seen Aimee?'

'Yeah I saw her go upstairs; I think she went to the toilet,' they said to Leyton.

Aimee had now been in the bathroom a few minutes and wiped away the tears. She fixed her makeup and took a deep breath. She opened the bathroom door and could hear, "Blinding Lights" by The Weeknd playing from the speakers. She was walking down the stairs at the same time Leyton was walking up; they met halfway. He could see that Aimee was upset and had possibly been crying, 'I'm sorry I shouldn't have said that,' he stood in front of her on the stairs.

Aimee cleared her throat, 'Why would you say those things?' she asked.

'I'm so sorry!' Leyton took Aimee's hand; she looked at him.

'I just want you, me and Kat to enjoy our

friendship, to never be distant,' she said.

'I know,' Leyton responded. He was now holding on to both of Aimee's hands, 'I just don't want you to waste your time, don't let him hold you back,' he said referring to Matt.

Aimee took a deep breath and pulled her hands away, 'Enjoy the rest of your evening, I have to go,' she said to Leyton and walked away.

It was now around 10.35pm; Kat sent a WhatsApp message to Aimee that she was on her way to the party and Aimee had not seen the message as her phone was in her clutch bag. Aimee was disappointed at the night she had, and her morale was very low. Matt was unreliable and she hadn't enjoyed talking to Leyton because of the things he had said, and she wasn't sure if Kat was coming to the party, so she had decided to head home.

She went to the rear garden to look for Matt and when she found him, she saw him slumped against the garden fence unable to keep his head up. 'I want to go home,' Aimee said to Matt, but he ignored her and shrugged his shoulders.

'Get a taxi then,' he responded, 'no one's stopping you.'

'Matt, you need to go home too, this isn't good,' Aimee said to him, concerned. She was kneeling on the grass as Matt was sitting on the grass with his back to the garden fence.

Aimee put her hand on Matt's shoulder as he suddenly got up and walked with his arms wide open towards Lewis. Lewis laughed and said, 'Mate you're a lightweight!', meanwhile in the party, the speakers were blasting "Wild Ones" by Flo Rida featuring Sia.

It was now 10.41pm and Kat had just arrived at Lewis's birthday party. After arriving and going through the hallway she looked around the house for Aimee, searching upstairs, downstairs, the living room, dining room and front garden - she didn't find Aimee. However she had not searched in the rear garden. Kat called

Aimee's phone but there was no response, so she simply assumed Aimee had gone home.

Kat then went to the kitchen/diner where she found cans and bottles of cider, cans and bottles of lager beer on the kitchen countertop. She took one to open; she was drinking alone, surrounded by the smell of alcohol and mixed drinks in the kitchen. Kat was leaning against the large marble kitchen island and facing the dining table, she was tapped on the shoulder by another girl. Kat turned round and looked at her, because of the loud music she leaned towards Kat's ear, 'Hi my name is Yas, nice to meet you!' the girl said raising her voice.

Kat smiled and introduced herself, they shook hands, 'Nice to meet you too,' Kat added. Yas had a pixie cut with dark hair and blue highlights and she was also holding a drink in her hand. She stood to the side of Kat, 'How do you know Lewis?' Kat asked Yas

'We are neighbours, I live next door, I

know his family quite well'.

'Oh, I see, cause when I saw you, I was sure you don't go to our college.'

'I don't go to any college, I am working at the moment,' said Yas, leaning into Kat's ear; the music in the kitchen coming through the speakers was quite loud. "Good Times" by Roll Deep featuring Jodie Connor was playing.

Kat smiled at Yas, 'Let's go to the living room it's a little quieter there,' said Yas, and they both left the kitchen and moved to the living room, sitting next to each other on a sofa. There was music playing in the background but at least they could hear each other when they spoke.

The living room lights were off, the only lighting was the ambient floor lamps at each corner of the living room, they were glowing pink and purple which gave the room a relaxed feel.

Yas was wearing a skinny fit ripped denim dungaree with a white crop top beneath; Kat was in a black tank top and army green camo print jeans.

Yas asked Kat, 'How long have you had your nose piercing?'

'Two years.'

'I really like it'.

'Thanks!'

At this moment Kat had just spotted Leyton as he was walking through the crowd of people in the living room, 'Sorry could you give me a sec?' she said to Yas, putting her hand on Yas' shoulder,

'Sure,' Yas replied politely.

Kat got up from the sofa and walked quickly to catch Leyton, she tapped him on the shoulder. He turned round, and they hugged, 'Have you been here long?' Kat asked.

'Been here since 8, I was just about to leave,' he replied, they were both now stood in the hallway. 'Have you seen Aimee?' Kat asked.

'She is outside in the back garden, she's

with Matt, don't think she's left yet,' said Leyton.

'Ok will say hi to her,' Kat replied. Leyton said goodbye to Kat and left the party. Kat went back to the living room and to the sofa to sit with Yas, 'Sorry,' she said to Yas.

'That's ok,' Yas smiled, 'so do you know most people here?' she asked Kat.

'Well, I know the birthday boy, Lewis, he's in my Psychology class, and my best friends Leyton and Aimee they were here, Leyton I was talking to earlier, other faces here I know from college,' said Kat.

There was a pause.

Kat was looking at Yas's neck, 'What?' Yas asked,

Kat replied, 'Your tattoo,' Yas moved closer to Kat on the sofa. Yas then tilted her head to one side allowing Kat to get a closer look of the tattoo on her neck. Kat leaned in and put her finger on Yas's neck tattoo, slowly moving her finger on Yas's skin. 'Do you have any other tattoos?' Kat asked.

Yas put forward her arm and showed Kat

the tattoo she had of a swan, 'And you?' Yas asked, Kat put her back to Yas and put aside her hair covering the back of her neck to reveal her dove tattoo, 'Can you see it?' she asked Yas.

'Yes, I love it' said Yas, they both then faced each other as they sat on the sofa, both holding their drinks.

'If you could go anywhere in the world, where would you go?' Kat asked,

Yas smiled and put her fingers over her lips, 'Well … if I could take you with me, it would be Mauritius.'

'Why?' Kat replied smiling,

'The night sky is beautiful, I would want you to witness it, you can just lay on the beach, any beach and admire the stars,' Yas and Kat continued talking.

Aimee had had enough for the evening so she came through the garden doors leading into the living room. As she stepped into the living room, she wanted to walk straight to the hallway to leave,

Aimee looked to her right and a few meters away saw Kat was kissing Yas on the sofa. Aimee chose not to say anything or interrupt their moment, even though she wanted to say goodnight to her best friend, '*I didn't even know she was here,*' Aimee thought to herself, as Aimee walked towards the hallway Kat saw her from the corner of her eye leaving. 'Be right back!' she said to Yas.

'Is something wrong?' Yas asked.

'No, I have just seen someone that's all,' said Kat. Kat followed Aimee who was now outside in front of the house waiting for her taxi. Kat walked up behind her as Aimee turned around and saw her. Kat could see a worried look on her friend's face, 'Aimee, hey what's wrong?' Kat asked. Aimee sighed looking away from Kat with her arms crossed.

Aimee shook her head. 'Nothing' she replied and Kat put her arms around Aimee's waist and faced her. 'I have had such a shit night,' Aimee said with her voice breaking, a tear streaking down her face. Kat hugged her, Aimee said to Kat 'Leyton said some things I thought he wouldn't say as a friend and Matt is ignoring me like I don't exist, he's a mess, I just want to go home.'

At this moment Yas had left the house party looking for Kat. Yas was outside the house and stood on the driveway looking ahead at Kat and Aimee who were on the street pavement at the front of the house, she could see Kat and Aimee meters away because the front gate was open. The taxi arrived to take Aimee home, she got inside, Kat stood at the rear door of the car, the car windows were down, Aimee said to Kat, 'I will call you later'.

'Let me know when you get home,' Kat replied. She felt agitated and turned round to see Yas standing on the driveway. Kat had her arms crossed as they walked to the front door of the house party and they said nothing to each other. Yas could sense that Kat's mood had changed.

Kat and Yas were now inside the house, stood in the hallway, the music still playing loudly and the sound of chatter from the party guests. Yas stood in front of Kat and put her hand on Kat's shoulder, 'Are you ok?' she asked and Kat sighed. 'You've got a face like thunder,' Yas added.

'Sorry I have to speak to someone,' said Kat and she turned away from Yas.

As she turned away Yas quickly pulled Kat back by the hand, 'Leave it, let's just enjoy the evening,' Yas said and moved closer proceeding to kiss Kat on the mouth, there was a pause.

'Sorry,' Kat replied and walked away, heading to the rear garden to look for Matt. Yas followed her.

Kat found Matt and others towards the side fence of the garden and when she approached Matt she pulled on his shoulder, 'Hey who do you think you are!?' she said to Matt, trying to get his attention.

Matt ignored her, 'Kat what do you want?' asked Lewis who was stood next to Matt.

'I wasn't talking to you,' she replied to

Lewis.

Lewis sniggered 'Are you serious right now?' he said to Kat.

Matt faced Kat and stood right in front of her, to her face. 'What has she told you now?' he said to Kat, slurring his words. Kat moved her head aside because of the strong smell of alcohol on Matt's breath, she shook her head.

'You're a joke - look at you!' Kat said to Matt. Most of the people in the rear garden stopped their conversations and turned towards Kat and Matt, the music stopped playing in the background.

'You don't even know where Aimee is right now,' she added, and crossed her arms. 'Why does she waste her time with you?' she said to Matt.

Matt laughed, Matt threw his can of beer towards Kat, and it poured over her face and clothes. She gasped in shock; furiously she rushed forward towards Matt. Others near them quickly ran towards them to stop the fight as Kat shoved Matt backwards into the garden fence. 'Are you mad?' he shouted and attempted to lunge back at Kat, they were quickly separated by others around them.

Matt's friends held him back, 'Come on mate let's get you home,' Lewis said.

As Matt stumbled leaving the garden with Lewis, he muttered, 'Nobody wants you here, get lost Kat, you prick'.

Lewis and friends opened the garden doors and walked with Matt to get him inside, Lewis jokingly said 'no more drinks for this man!'

For a few seconds Kat looked down towards the grass in the garden with her hands on her hips, she turned round and saw Yas; Yas's arms were crossed in disappointment, Yas shook her head.

Kat sighed, 'Yas I am sor...' Yas walked away from Kat and left the garden to go inside.

Now Matt had left the party and was

outside the house leaning against the gate waiting for his taxi to arrive; he was drunk and got out his phone and sent a message to Lucy, *'cum and spend time wit me I muss u'*. Lucy had chosen not to attend the birthday party and that evening she was in bed when Matt sent the message. She woke up opened her phone and looked at the text message, not bothering to respond, and went back to sleep, ignoring it. He then sent another message, this time to Aimee, *'U need to sort ur friend out'*. in the meanwhile the taxi carrying Aimee arrived at 49 Faircroft Road Reigate. Aimee sent a WhatsApp message to Kat, *'got home fine'.* She saw the message from Matt and ignored it, she came through the front door into the hallway.

Jerome was in the living room and had fallen asleep on the sofa, he was woken up by the sound of the front door, 'Aimee you, ok?' he asked.

'Yes,' she responded.

'How was the party?' Jerome asked. Aimee was too upset and didn't respond. She walked upstairs and went to her bedroom, shut the door and sat on her bed. She sighed as Jerome knocked on Aimee's bedroom door. 'Aimee?' he said standing at the door.

'I don't want to talk about it sorry I just want to be left alone,' she replied.

'Ok' he said and went back downstairs.

A few minutes later Jerome came to Aimee's bedroom door, 'I've made hot chocolate for you if want, it's at the door, goodnight.' he said and went to bed.

The next day was Sunday, it was the afternoon, 12.34pm. Aimee was sat in the living room looking at her phone, she had five missed calls from Kat and a few seconds later Kat rang again. Aimee picked up the phone and answered the call, there was silence on the call for a few seconds.

Kat said, 'I am sorry' with a low tone, 'Aimz talk to me.'

Aimee responded, 'I don't know what to say,' there was a pause .... 'I'm sorry for what he did, but he's so angry, you embarrassed him in front of everyone!'

Kat said, 'You know he was in the wrong and he was out of control.'

Aimee replied, 'You're both making it really difficult for me, how can I spend time with both of you if you hate each other?' Aimee put her head in her hand with her face in the palm of her hand.

'I will always be there for you Aimz.'

'I know,' there was a long pause.

'Sorry I don't want to talk about this anymore.'

Kat replied, 'That's ok, I understand.' Aimee ended the call; she laid down on the sofa looking up at the ceiling. Aimee was worried about how long this will continue in her life, how long would she have to keep Matt and Kat apart, whilst staying close to both of them.

DECEMBER

It was early December on a Tuesday in the evening, Matt went to over to the Stearman household which was Lucy's parents' house. He wanted to meet up with Lucy as she had promised a few weeks earlier to help him with Further Maths. Matt knocked on the front door and Lucy's mum opened the door and gave him a warm embrace, 'Please come in, Matt.' Matt stood in the hallway, 'How is your mum; how is Lorraine?' Lucy's mum asked.

Matt replied, 'She's ok thanks for asking.'

'Well let me take your jacket, Lucy is upstairs,' she said to Matt. Matt went upstairs to Lucy's bedroom, her bedroom door was slightly open, he knocked and then opened the door.

'Hello stranger,' was the response from Lucy. She was sat on the bed, Lucy was wearing a grey crop top and grey leggings.

A few minutes later Matt and Lucy were both sat on the bed opposite each other, books spread over the bed as they revised together and exchanged notes, paying attention to the textbooks in front of them.

Half an hour later Matt looked up and smiled at Lucy briefly, she caught his gaze, 'What?' she asked.

'I didn't say anything,' Matt replied, and he continued reading the textbook.

Lucy closed the textbook she was holding and looked at Matt, 'So do you think you could do a 10K run like your dad?' she asked.

'Well, yes, I think so.'

'Really?' Lucy asked with a hint of sarcasm.

'Well, I do keep fit' Matt replied, 'try to work out' he added.

'Sure, you do' Lucy said, there was a pause as Lucy moved the books on the bed aside and moved forward closer to Matt. She proceeded to touch his arm and feel his muscles through his clothes, 'Hmm, ok I guess,' she said smirking.

Matt looked at Lucy's hair, he put his fingers through the side of her hair and moved her hair behind the ears, 'Has your hair always been that colour?' he asked.

'No' Lucy said shaking her head, 'before, it was blonde' she added.

'Really?'

'Yes'

'Do you have any pictures?' Matt asked, Lucy sat next to him on the bed, she put her hand on his thigh and he could smell her perfume which he liked, she brought out her phone and showed him older pictures from her phone gallery of when she was previously blonde.

'Can I ask you a personal question?' Lucy said, Matt was looking at her lips. 'Why don't you talk to your dad?' she asked.

Matt looked away as if fed up with the conversation, 'Why do you want to know?' he said to Lucy, she looked into his eyes. 'I call him maybe once a month, or he calls me, no substance to our conversations to be honest,' Matt replied.

'And do you stay with him in Bath?'

Matt replied, 'I did recently for a couple of days, erm it was strange.'

'What do you mean?'

Matt replied, 'Well his new girlfriend, she's unpredictable, when I stayed with them it was awkward, she's wild - the way she was looking at me, and she was constantly saying to us *let's do something fun*, or she couldn't hold a conversation steadily longer than a few minutes'.

Matt rolled his eyes and added, 'She was agitated, sometimes restless, I think she was on something. I didn't want to say anything to upset my dad, because meeting his new girlfriend was me accepting, he had moved on from my mum,' there was a pause.

'Even when we went for dinner the three of us, she was laughing at things that were not funny or flirting with everyone. I mean I see why my dad is into her, but she is the complete opposite of my mum,' Matt said to Lucy.

Lucy put her hand on his knee, 'Matt as long as you are still speaking to him that is what's important, some people our age don't even hear from their dads anymore' Lucy said.

Lucy got up from the bed to open the bedroom window, Matt asked her, 'You had a party here during the summer for your birthday, how was it?' she looked at him and said.

'It was terrible, I actually want to go to Paris for my birthday next year, I won't celebrate it here, you can join us for my birthday weekend, we are taking the Eurostar, I would like you to be there'.

'Sure,' Matt replied.

Lucy added, 'Plus my friend Salina is going to be there, I saw the way you were looking at her at Lewis birthday last year'.

Matt and Lucy were both standing by the bedroom window, 'Next year by September I will be off to LSE and you will miss me,' Lucy said to Matt smiling at him,

Matt sniggered, 'You seem quite sure about LSE; LSE is not easy to get into, they get a high number of applications.' Matt then moved closer to Lucy standing face to face with her, 'and I certainly won't miss you, anyway what would you study?' he added.

'BSc in Econometrics and Mathematical Economics, that's my target,' said Lucy.

'Hmm ok …. but are you studying it because you want to or because someone has told you to?' Matt asked, there was a pause.

Lucy replied, 'You mean my dad? I don't make my life decisions for his benefit, but also, I want to be in London, the social scene in Surrey is non-existent.'

Lucy added, 'Longer term I would want to settle in Paris.'

'What's great about Paris?' Matt sniggered, Lucy looked at him in the eye, she put her hand on his arm.

'Have you ever kissed a French guy?' she asked Matt with a raised eyebrow.

'No, I don't do that' Matt said with a confused look.

'Then you won't understand,' replied Lucy smiling, she looked out the window.

'And for you?' she asked Matt.

'It's complicated, the plan is to go to the same uni as Aimee'.

'How spontaneous,' Lucy said sarcastically, there was a pause ....

'What happened between you and Lewis?' Matt asked.

'Why do you want to know?'

'Lewis says you were too clingy, so he ended things,' said Matt and Lucy smiled.

'Lewis says a lot of things, do you believe

him or me?' she replied, Lucy placed her hands on his chest and looked at Matt, she said to him, raising her eyebrows, 'Does it bother you that I used to be with Lewis? When Lewis and I were together I saw the way you used to look at me?'

'I'm over that now,' Matt replied, he added 'Shall we get on with it? Linear Regression and Correlation'

'Sounds good' Lucy replied nodding, they sat back on the bed opposite each other and re-opened the Further Maths revision and practice textbook, they continued to study statistics for another 2 hours, then Matt headed home.

A few days later, a Friday evening around 7.16pm, Aimee, Matt and Lewis were at a tenpin bowling alley in Redhill Surrey; the multilane bowling chain they were at also had an on-site bar & diner, a dedicated games area and arcade.

Earlier in the evening Matt had suggested to Aimee that they should go bowling and then invited Lewis at the last minute. They were at the reception of the bowling lanes, music was playing in the venue, "Jumpin Jumpin" by Destiny's Child in the background, they changed their footwear to the bowling shoes provided by the venue.

Lewis was glancing at Aimee. Aimee was not smiling and had her arms crossed whilst standing as they waited for their lane to be prepared. They went to bowling Lane 6, Matt stepped up first to bowl picking up a bowling ball and releasing it knocking down 5 pins. There was a smell of leather and polished wood in the air. As Matt was bowling, Lewis approached Aimee. 'Can I ask you a question?' he said as he leaned towards her with a smirk, 'So is Kat seeing someone then?' he asked. Aimee didn't respond. 'Tell me' Lewis added.

'I don't know'.

'You do,' he smiled, 'you're her friend, does

she like guys?' Lewis asked.

'What do you mean?'

Lewis added, 'Well at my house party, I heard she got quite close with….'

'Why don't you ask her?' Aimee said in frustration, 'you should talk to her yourself,' she added.

Matt walked back towards Lewis and Aimee, 'You're up mate,' he said to Lewis and Lewis stepped up to bowl. A few meters behind the bowling lane approach, there was a round wooden table and leather seats fitted around it. Matt walked away to go to the toilet, he had left his phone on the wooden table, as he approached the toilets Matt realised he forgot his mobile phone and went back to the table. Aimee picked up his phone as it had vibrated and she wanted to open it, as Matt walked back to the table he saw her holding his phone, 'What are you doing going through my phone?' he said to Aimee.

'Nothing, nothing sorry,' she responded,

and quickly gave the phone back to him, Matt took it and proceeded to head to the toilet.

Lewis walked back, leaving the bowling lane, he turned to Aimee, 'You are next,' he said to her, Aimee got up and approached the bowling lane. She stepped into the lane releasing the bowling ball, it moved perfectly in the middle down the lane and she hit a strike, Lewis nodded his head in surprise, Aimee didn't smile.

Whilst Matt was in the toilet, there was an awkward silence between Aimee and Lewis, Aimee tried not to make eye contact with him, Lewis kept looking at her as they sat opposite each other.

'What did you say to Kat at my birthday that she reacted that way?' he asked Aimee. He added, 'You said to Kat that Matt's been giving you grief or something? She was an embarrassment.'

Aimee replied, 'Kat can make her own decisions.'

Lewis asked Aimee, 'Do you have a

problem with me?'

Aimee sighed and rolled her eyes. 'I don't'.

'Well fix your attitude then,' Lewis replied and that comment annoyed Aimee.

She turned to Lewis and said 'Lewis why don't you fu...' before Aimee could finish, she felt a hand on her shoulder,

Matt had returned from the toilet, 'You ok?' he asked Aimee. Aimee said nothing, Lewis smiled. Aimee had her arms crossed and legs crossed, 'did I miss something?' Matt asked.

'Nothing all good' Lewis replied, they continued bowling for another 40 minutes.

After bowling they sat at a booth in the Diner of the Bowling centre, Matt sitting next to Aimee and Lewis opposite to them, 'It's been fun, but I have to go,' said Lewis. 'Aren't you going to stay and order food?' Matt asked.

'No I will see you later,' Lewis replied. Lewis got up and proceeded to shake Matt's hand and left for the exit.

Matt turned to Aimee and said, 'Look I am sorry about last week, when I was shouting at you, I shouldn't have done that!'

'I don't like it when you get so upset over the smallest things,' Aimee replied. There was a pause.

Matt said to Aimee, 'You told me before that when Jerome and your mum argue it gets heated, I remember when my parents did that before they split up, I would put the pillows over my ears whist I was in my bedroom, just to stop hearing them argue.' Matt held Aimee's hand, she leaned in to kiss him on the cheek, he kissed her on the forehead.

A waiter came to their booth for their food order, he stood with a pen and notepad, 'Hi what would you like to order? We have burgers, nachos, noodles, wraps and salad,' said the waiter.

'I will have the beef burger please', said Matt, he proceeded to scroll down the menu with his fingers '...with mac and cheese.' he added.

Aimee followed up, 'Can I go with the cheese and bacon beef burger with mac & cheese,' she said.

'Er …. are you sure?' Matt asked looking at Aimee. A hesitant look crossed Aimee's face.

'Sorry can you give us a minute?' Matt said to the waiter.

'Sure' he responded and walked away.

'What's wrong?' Aimee asked Matt.

'Well, the calories, there's a lot of calories in that babe, maybe you want something lighter.' Matt replied, there was a pause and Aimee nodded her head once and looked down at the table, Matt gestured to the waiter who was walking back towards them.

'Why do you do that?' Aimee asked Matt.

'What do you mean?' replied Matt; the waiter returned and Matt said to the waiter, 'I will have the beef burger with mac and cheese', the waiter then turned to Aimee.

Aimee sighed, 'I will have the salad,' she said without making eye contact with the waiter.

'Sure?' the waiter asked.

'Yes,' Aimee responded with a low voice.

As the waiter walked away, Matt said to Aimee, 'Look I can change it back to the burger for you?' Aimee was silent. 'Well say something then' Matt added.

Aimee shook her head, 'Well how come you can have, eat whatever you want?' she asked.

'But I'm working out,' Matt replied, 'it was you that mentioned it before, that you want to watch what you eat babe,' he added.

'When did I say that?' Aimee replied in frustration, she got up and decided to go to the toilet, when she got to the toilet, she looked in the mirror at herself. In her mind she was trying to reassure herself that Matt loved her and his behaviour will change. She finished in the toilet and came back to the table, they sat down and ate together, when they left the bowling venue, they took the bus together to make their way home.

When Aimee got home, she took off her coat in the hallway and was heading to the stairs, 'Aimee!' her mum shouted from the kitchen, Aimee sighed and went to the kitchen, she saw in the kitchen her mum had ordered take away fish and chips for everyone. Jerome, Emma and Tom were all sat at the dining table, Emma got up and hugged Aimee, 'Sweetheart have some, here is yours' she said to Aimee.

Aimee replied, 'I'm ok thanks I don't want to eat that,' Jerome and Emma looked at each other in surprise for a second, 'You've always loved a fry up,' Emma said to her daughter.

Aimee replied, 'Well maybe it's time for a change.' Aimee walked away and went to her bedroom.

A few minutes later Emma knocked on Aimee's bedroom door and came into Aimee's room, the bedroom lights were off, but the bedside table lamp was on, dimly lit, 'Your mood is off and I can tell something is bothering you,' said Emma.

Aimee sat on her bed with her back to the headboard, Emma sat next to her on the bed, there was a pause, Emma sighed, 'Ok I am just going to say it, has he said anything to you about your weight?' there was a short pause and she looked at her mum. Emma held Aimee's left hand, 'I know you sweetheart.'

Aimee cleared her throat, 'He made a comment about how he can eat certain foods and I can't, he can eat what he wants because he works out and I don't. What pisses me off is he said I told him I want to watch what I eat and I never said that.'

Emma said to her, 'Aimee listen to me and I am only going to say this once, never let a man make decisions for you, or tell you what you should or shouldn't eat, never, no matter how much you think you love him'. Emma got up from the bed and opened the bedroom door, as she looked back at her daughter, she whispered, 'I will keep your chippy in the fridge,' and smiled closing the door.

It was the next day, Saturday, in the afternoon, Aiden Stearman, Lucy's dad, heard a knock at the front door and he went to the hallway, and he opened the front door, it was Matt at the door.

'Hi Mr Stearman,' Matt said.

'Matt please come in,' they both stood in the hallway, 'I am not sure if Lucy is in, you wanted to see her right?' Aiden asked.

'Oh, yes,' Matt replied.

Aiden moved up the staircase, 'Lucy !?' there was no response, 'No she's gone out so I will let her know you came round,' he said to Matt.

As Aiden was standing facing Matt, he asked 'Matt you're studying Economics, right?'

'Yes, I am' Matt replied.

'What do you want to do after Economics, after your A-Levels?'

'I want to look at M&A maybe Accounting'.

'Your dad said you're planning to study Economics at Uni as well, have you decided on that?'

'Yes.'

'Ok, is that with a placement year Matt?' Aiden asked, Matt nodded.

'Come into the living room,' said Aiden. Aiden stood by the fireplace,

Aiden said to Matt, 'Well look, we have an M&A team, accounting team and an internship program at Cedar Capstone Investments, in the city where your dad and I worked. Well, we don't work together anymore, he left as you know, but you've been to the offices once before in Bishopsgate right?'

'Yes, I have' Matt replied.

'Good well Matt I have spoken to HR a few days ago, if you want to get the placement year just let me know I can arrange it,' said Aiden.

'Really Mr Stearman?'

'Please call me Aiden.'

'That's brilliant I don't know what to say.' Matt said smiling.

Aiden said to Matt, 'Don't mention it, it would be great for your CV, I ran it past your dad last week, we are doing great things at the company, you will learn a lot in M&A, then when you finish your degree, you can get on the Graduate Rotation Programme I will make sure.'

'Thank you!'

'No worries, just let me know when ok, anything else?' Aiden asked standing with his hands in his trouser pockets.

'No.'

'Ok see you soon, I will let Lucy know you dropped by.'

Matt left the living room, headed to the hallway, and left the house via the front door.

A few days later Lorraine, upon hearing her about son's internship offer, came to visit Aiden, she knocked on the front door of the house, after waiting a minute, she rang the doorbell. Aiden opened the front door, he was wearing a white and blue striped shirt, beige khaki trousers. 'Evening Lorraine,' he said standing in the door, 'is everything ok?' he asked her.

'Can I come in?'

'Yes, come in please' said Aiden, Lorraine stood in the hallway opposite Aiden.

'Would you like anything to drink?' Aiden asked,

'I won't be staying long thanks.'

'How can I help you?'

'I came to talk to you about Matt,' said Lorraine, there was a short pause.

'Look, thank you for the internship offer during his degree, I appreciate it,' her arms crossed as she stood, Aiden smiled knowing what was coming next.

'But?'

'But I don't want him to take it Aiden.'

'O....... k...' Aiden responded with a slightly confused look.

Lorraine proceeded to say, 'He can find his own way, I want him to work for something, he's had everything handed to him on a plate, it's not personal, he needs to try and find something, so he knows what hard work feels like.'

Aiden cleared his throat and put his hand in front of him to gesture to Lorraine to stop talking, that she did not need to say more but Lorraine continued, 'His father gave him everything easily, I don't want him going down that path of being overprivileged,' she added.

Aiden smiled and put his hands on his waist, 'Are you going to tell him Lorraine?' Aiden asked.

'In my own time,' replied Lorraine, Aiden nodded his head.

'You sure you don't want a drink?'

'I'm fine,' Lorraine replied, Aiden turned away from her to go to the living room then paused, he turned back round to Lorraine.

'You know when you take something away

from someone, it usually tends to push them away,' he said with a smirk.

Aiden added, 'Perhaps you're getting a little carried away, it's just an internship with first-hand experience of financial services.'

Lorraine picked up her handbag and headed to the front door.

'Thanks for your time anyway,' said Lorraine and she walked out, leaving the house.

It was a Thursday, in the afternoon, Kat had come round to see Aimee and to also apologise for a recent argument they had; she had cupcakes to hand in a gift box and knocked on the front door of 49 Faircroft Road. Jerome opened the front door and smiled, 'Oh are those cupcakes for me?' he said, he could see the cupcakes through the transparent cover of the giftbox.

Kat smiled, 'No sorry they are for Aimee,' she said.

He nodded, 'Right then she's upstairs,

come in.' Kat moved to the staircase and walked up, she knocked on Aimee's bedroom room door, Aimee was sat on her bed.

Kat walked into the bedroom, she stood holding the gift box, 'Aimz I am sorry for how I behaved with Matt and I don't want to make things difficult for you,' Aimee had her arms crossed whilst looking at Kat, who sat on the bedside. Kat slowly placed the box of cupcakes on Aimee's bed she then opened the box, Aimee saw a Vanilla Cherry Bakewell Cupcake, Chocolate Blackforest Cupcake, Vanilla 99 Flake Cupcake , Peanut Butter Cookie and Apple Danish, there was a pause.

'Is that a smile?' Kat said and Aimee couldn't help but smile slightly and then they hugged. They then sat on the bedside next to each other, holding hands and with their foreheads touching, leaning against each other, there was a moment of quiet.

'I don't like it when we argue, and I do care about you,' Kat said to Aimee. Aimee put her hand on Kat's thigh.

Aimee picked up the Chocolate Blackforest Cupcake and started to eat it, 'Oh that's so good,' she said to Kat, 'You always know how to make me smile with food,' Aimee added.

Kat picked up a cupcake to eat.

'By the way you were great in the play, amazing, so alive, I couldn't take my eyes off you,' Aimee said to Kat, 'you really seem to enjoy acting,' she added.

Kat smiled, 'Thanks,' she said, Kat put down her cupcake and faced Aimee.

'Aimz, look there was something I wanted to tell you, my uncle wants me to join him in Tenerife for the whole of next summer, to help with running his bar, erm it's going to be for 2 or 3 months, I haven't made the decision yet, but really wanted you know. We will still go on our holiday to Marbella, I promise.'

Aimee nodded her head slowly taking in what Kat said, 'Family is important. If you want to, you should spend time with your uncle,' she said to Kat with a smile of reassurance. They spent the rest of the afternoon and evening together. Kat also chose to stay and have dinner in the Larkson household with Aimee, Tom, and Jerome.

December 20th and it was now approaching Christmas time. Aimee spoke to her mum and suggested that for Christmas Kat should stay with them, and Emma agreed with no hesitation, 'Invite her over and we'll talk about it,' Emma said to Aimee. Kat came over to the Larkson household to meet Emma and Aimee, Aimee opened the front door and hugged her. It was cold outside and snowing. Kat came into the living room, Aimee and Kat sat next to each other on the sofa while Emma sat opposite them.

'Would you like something to drink.... tea?' Emma asked.

'Lemon and Ginger tea please,' Kat replied.

Jerome also came downstairs into the living room and sat next to Emma, 'It's really good to see you again Kat,' Jerome said to her. Emma got up and went to the kitchen, she switched on the electric kettle, she returned to the living room a minute later.

Emma looked at Jerome and then at Aimee and smiled, she then faced Kat, 'Well we've all spoken about it as a family, and we would really love it if you stayed with us for Christmas Kat, please. We don't want you to spend Christmas alone,' said Emma. Aimee took Kat by the hand.

Kat had her mouth open for a few seconds not knowing what to say, she nodded her head, 'Thank you I didn't see that coming,' she responded.

'It's our pleasure, and please stay for dinner,' said Jerome.

Two days later the morning of December 22nd Emma and Aimee left the house; they got into the car on the driveway. Emma's intention was to drive to pick up Kat. Aimee was sitting in the passenger's seat; they waited in the car for a few minutes to allow the windscreen to defrost due to the cold weather and Emma wiped the snow from the car windows and mirrors, and they started their journey. Kat lived in a flat which was a 12-minute walk from the Larkson house. When they arrived, they saw Kat outside the front door of the flat, standing with her suitcase. Emma parked the car and stepped out of the car; she hugged Kat, Kat then put her suitcase in the boot of the car. Kat sat in the back seat.

Emma drove her daughter and Kat back to the Larkson house, they arrived, and Emma parked in the driveway.

Aimee took Kat's suitcase from the car boot, Emma opened the front door with her keys, Kat came through the front door, she walked into the hallway, turned to her right looking into the living room. Jerome had his feet up on the coffee table watching television, Jerome waved at Kat and with a smile said, 'Welcome'.

'Thanks,' Kat replied, she went upstairs to Aimee's bedroom.

It was Christmas Eve 11.23pm in the Larkson household. Aimee and Kat were sat on the living room sofa opposite each other, the living room lights were dimly lit, there was a smell of mulled wine in the living room coming from the kitchen. The Christmas tree lights flickering were illuminating the living room; both Aimee and Kat were in their pyjamas, the television was on and the volume low, everyone else had gone to sleep.

Aimee looked at Kat and asked Kat, 'Do you still think about your dad?'

Kat took a deep breath, there was a pause she looked at the Christmas tree, Kat replied, 'Much less but I remember the day very well. That afternoon, I remember I was on the sofa, my mum on the left of me, dad on the right, the police knocking on the front door. They came in and spoke to my dad, he looked sad, they put his hands behind his back and arrested him. It's strange we were just watching a film together on TV and laughing, next thing he's in handcuffs.'

Aimee held Kat's hands; Kat added, 'I didn't know what was going on at that time, but now that I know I try not think about what he did, and I don't think I can look at him knowing what he did.' Kat took a breath and slumped her head, putting her face in the palm of her hands, she said to Aimee, 'All my mum just says is that it was a dark time in his past but she's never admitted what he did was wrong, and I have never been able to get my head round it,' Kat cleared her throat. 'To think the same hands he used to look after me he also used to abuse others,' Kat added, she shook her head.

'Have you tried to visit him; do you know where he is?' Aimee asked.

'I know he's in Belmarsh. When I was younger, I was angry at myself for allowing them to take him away; when they arrested him, I felt so powerless, like a bad dream where you can't move. I wanted to release him from the handcuffs and run away with him.'

'I'm sorry,' replied Aimee, Kat smiled slightly, Aimee wanted to lift the mood, she took Kat by the hand, out of the living room and to the kitchen which leads to the garden, the kitchen was dimly lit with a small source of light coming from the hallway and the moonlight shining onto a section of the kitchen floor. Aimee opened a large stainless steel cooking pot which was on the cooker hob and poured mulled wine from the pot into two mugs using a large spoon, a cinnamon stick and orange slice was showing at the top of their mugs, the mulled wine was warm as Emma had cooked it earlier.

Aimee opened the kitchen drawer and took out a tray of Ferrero Rocher. Aimee held the tray of chocolates and Kat held both mugs of the mulled wine. Aimee opened and pulled to the side the aluminium and glass sliding doors to the garden, the cold air came into the kitchen from the garden and Kat felt how cold it was, she shuddered, 'It's cold!'

'Wait,' Aimee said, Aimee quickly went upstairs and took two thick long sleeve bathrobes, two swimsuits, she also took two towels.

She came back downstairs to the kitchen and gave Kat a bathrobe, swimsuit, and towel and they stepped into the garden. There was no electric lighting in the garden but there was moonlight so from the garden patio they walked to the jacuzzi. Aimee took the cover off, 'When did you get a jacuzzi?' Kat asked.

'Jerome got it last week,' said Aimee, both Kat and Aimee took off their pyjamas, 'Ah its cold,' said Kat.

'You can get changed in the shed,' Aimee said to Kat, who took the bathrobe and swimsuit with her and ran to the garden shed to get changed. Aimee turned on the hot tub and put on her wireless Bluetooth speakers, placing them on the decking next to the hot tub. The radio was playing "Frosty The Snowman" by Ella Fitzgerald.

Kat stepped into the hot tub holding her cup of mulled wine, 'Oh that's better,' Kat said as she took a sip of the mulled wine and then put it down by the side of the jacuzzi. There was blue LED mood lighting in the hot tub giving the water an ambient glow. Aimee was in the middle of the hot tub and Kat moved slowly behind her and put her arms around Aimee's waist, leaning her chin on Aimee's shoulder; she kissed the back of Aimee's neck and Kat then tried to playfully nibble on Aimee's earlobe; Aimee moved her head away smiling.

'What do you want for next year?' Kat asked Aimee.

Aimee replied, 'For Matt and I to be happier, to get into the Uni of my choice and for Jerome and mum to stop bickering.'

'And you, what do you want?'

Kat paused then replied, 'To stop pushing people into garden fences!' They both laughed loudly and drank the rest of their mulled wine, enjoying another hour together in the jacuzzi.

JANUARY

It was a Monday evening around 6.20pm, Aimee was at home downstairs in the living room sitting on the sofa watching television; "*The Simpsons*" was on. Aimee was sitting comfortably wearing a grey t-shirt and white joggers when she heard a loud bang upstairs as if a heavy object was dropped to the floor, then she heard Jerome and Emma starting to argue. She looked up at the ceiling - she could hear their voices shouting over each other aggressively, and she picked up the remote control and muted the television. Aimee got off the sofa and put her feet on the carpeted floor, '*What now?*' Aimee thought to herself. She went to the hallway and started walking up the stairs, and as she reached the top of the stairs her stepfather Jerome opened the bedroom door furiously shouting, 'No Emma I'm done!' He walked past Aimee and rushed downstairs, he was wearing a navy-blue hoodie and navy-blue joggers. Jerome got his jacket from the coat rack in the hallway and put on his trainers, he took some keys with him and opened the front door, closed it with a bang and walked to the driveway where the car was parked. He went to the car which was his Renault Kadjar, it was dark outside but the front door security light came on so there was some visibility from the front door to the driveway. When Jerome sat in the car, in the driver's seat, he pushed the STOP/START button and turned the engine on sighing heavily. Aimee left the house and came out to meet him at the driveway, she stood at the car window on the driver's side and Jerome turned to look at her. He saw the worried look on her face as he stepped out of the car and gave her a hug. 'Don't leave,' Aimee said, they hugged for a few more seconds.

Jerome said to Aimee, 'Sorry, sweetheart I can't be around your mum right now it's not good for us!'

'What happened?' Aimee asked, Jerome shook his head.

He replied, 'I don't want to talk about it, I love you,' he said.

'Love you too,' she replied and Jerome opened the car's front door on the driver side and sat down; he put his seatbelt on, wound down the driver door window to speak to Aimee, 'I will text you where I will be staying Aimz,' he said to her.

'Ok' Aimee replied as Jerome drove the car past the driveway and to the electric front gates, which opened, Aimee then stood on the driveway with her arms crossed.

Aimee's younger brother Tom had come downstairs from his bedroom and was watching the driveway from the window of the living room. As Aimee came back into the house and closed the front door, she sighed and leaned back against the inside front door, Tom came to the front door standing in front of Aimee and he asked her, 'What's wrong?' with a worried look.

'It's ok,' Aimee said to her brother. She then added, 'Jerome will be staying somewhere else for a while, I don't know when he will be back.'

Aimee went upstairs into her parents' bedroom, the door was slightly open. She fully opened the bedroom door slowly as she heard her mum sobbing, upon opening the bedroom door she found the chest of drawers and the bedside table lamp on the floor and a broken tea mug. Emma was in a lace trim camisole night dress and was in tears sitting on the bedside. Aimee held her mum by the hand sitting next to her on the bedside, and put her other hand on her mums back. There was silence for half a minute and then Emma sighed, 'I messed up,' she said to Aimee. 'I don't want to lose him,' Emma added, she was sobbing. They embraced and held each other closely; Aimee could feel her mum's tears on her cheek.

'Did he hurt you?' Aimee asked.

Emma shook her head. 'No' she responded, 'he's just angry, we need some time apart.' As Aimee got up to get tissues, Emma pulled her by the hand and looked at her eye to eye.

'Don't tell Tom about any of this and I don't want him to see all this,' she said to Aimee.

Emma said to her daughter, 'It's just all escalated, he's just found out he is going to be made redundant. We've been arguing and then he's seen a message on my phone which he's taken the wrong way'.

There was a pause.

'Let me clear this up' Aimee replied.

'Leave it,' Emma said to her daughter, Aimee saw the broken mug on the floor and lifted it, 'Mum did he throw this at you?' Aimee asked. Emma shook her head, Aimee left the bedroom and got some tissues for her mum, she then went downstairs and got a glass of water from the kitchen.

When Aimee came back upstairs and sat on the bedside next to Emma, she asked her mum, 'What happened?'

Emma replied, 'When the time is right, I will be ready to tell you what happened tonight, listen to me sweetheart....' Emma took a deep breath, 'Never keep secrets; be honest and find a way to work it out, if there is something on your mind talk about it.' There was another pause and Emma asked her daughter, 'Are you and Matt still ok?'

'Yes,' said Aimee.

Emma replied, 'I know he seems to care about you but the moment you are worried tell me, don't keep it in.'

Emma put back the lamp on the bedside table and put back the chest of drawers which had fallen to the floor, Aimee tidied up the rest of the room.

FEBRUARY

Three weeks later, a Thursday afternoon 5.34 pm, Aimee had come back home from college, she opened the front door with her keys and hung her coat in the hallway. She turned to the right into the living room to see Jerome and Emma sat next to each other; they were on the sofa, sitting quietly. Aimee had been listening to music and took off her earphones, the sound of "Someone You Loved" by Lewis Capaldi playing in her earphones. Emma was looking down at the coffee table motionless, Jerome said calmly, 'Aimee, please can you call your brother downstairs.'

'Why what's wrong?' Aimee asked, Jerome did not respond. There was a sad expression on both her parents faces. Aimee went upstairs, her heart was racing thinking her parents were ending their relationship. She didn't want to think about Jerome or Emma leaving her, especially after she lost her father years ago, as she reached the top of the stairs she called for her brother, 'Tom!' no response, she walked up to his bedroom door and knocked and entered. He quickly closed his laptop whilst he was sat on the bed.

'What is it?' he said to his sister taking off his headphones.

Tom was in his boxers and sat on the bedside, 'Tom come downstairs,' Aimee said to him.

'For what?'

'It's important,' Aimee replied and he sighed but before getting out of the bed said to his sister, 'Ok can you leave the room give me some privacy?'

Tom and Aimee came downstairs and sat next to each other on the opposite sofa as they faced Jerome and Emma, their parents were holding each other's hands, 'Your gran has had an accident, we need to go to the hospital to see her,' Jerome said, 'She is at St George's' he added.

'Is she gonna be ok?' Tom asked and there was a pause.

Jerome put his hand behind Emma's back to comfort her, 'I hope so,' Jerome replied. 'Put your shoes on, get changed and let's go. We may be there a while.' Jerome added.

Tom and Aimee went upstairs to get changed quickly while Jerome and Emma left the house, walked to the driveway, and sat in the car. A few minutes later Aimee and her brother left the house, Aimee locked the front door and with her brother went to join Jerome and Emma in the car. Both Aimee and Tom sat in the back of the car. Aimee looked at her phone and saw two missed calls from Matt. Emma sat in the front driver seat, Jerome in the front passenger seat. The plan was to drive to St George's Hospital so Emma put into the satellite navigation the address SW17

0QT, which showed a 45-minute drive from their location.

Five minutes into the drive to the hospital, Aimee's mobile phone vibrated with a notification, she saw a text message from Matt,

'WHY DIDN'T YOU PICK UP?' the message read. Aimee ignored the text message, as Emma drove to the hospital there was silence in the car. Aimee was worried, Tom even held her hand briefly in the car as he sensed she was upset.

Aimee replied to Matt via WhatsApp *'Gran had an accident we are going to St George's A&E.'* Aimee then put her phone on silent mode.

After a 57-minute drive, due to traffic, they reached St George's hospital. Emma parked the car at the visitors parking, then they all got out of the car.

They arrived at the entrance of St George's hospital and all of them picked up the disposable face masks at the entrance,

Aimee applied the hand sanitizer which was also available. There was a strong smell of alcohol, ethanol, coming from the hand sanitizer which dried quickly on Aimee's hands. They went to the reception of the hospital and were told to go to the

1st floor, St James Wing, to the Intensive Care Unit.

Once they arrived at the ICU, they were asked to go to a waiting room. After waiting for a few minutes the doctor sat the family down and took time to explain what had happened. She explained in the room to the family that June, who is Emma's mum and Aimee's grandmother, had a fall on the stairs and was injured. June had suffered a blow to the head, a fracture with bleeding around her brain. As this was a traumatic brain injury, they had operated in neurosurgery to stop the bleeding and June was in a stable condition after the surgery, but she was now in a coma. The doctor further explained that June's neighbour had overhead the sound of the fall and went next door to check on her, alerting emergency services immediately. After the family left the waiting room, they walked to the intensive care wards, Emma went inside the ward with Aimee who was holding her mother's hand.

A nurse took Emma and Aimee through to the ward June was in and once Emma saw her mother lying unconscious on the bed with a neck brace and tubes to help her breathe, she gasped, overwhelmed by what she saw Emma put her hand over her mouth. Emma moved closer and cried as she held her mothers' hand while standing at the bed side. 'Mum it's going to be ok,' Emma said to June with her voice breaking as she watched her mother motionless on the ventilator. Aimee put her hand on Emma's back to comfort her mother.

Jerome and Tom sat in the waiting area on the purple plastic chairs; Jerome put his arm around Tom to show that he cared, even though they said nothing to each other; Tom just looked to the floor. A few minutes later Tom also came to June's bedside to see his grandmother, Jerome then came to join them and offer his emotional support.

An hour later Aimee was alone with June and by June's bedside, Aimee held her grandmother's frail hand as she reflected on the memories they had. Tears flowed down from Aimee's eyes over her face; she wiped the tears with her hand. Aimee was sat on a chair by June's side with the back of the chair facing the door of the ward. Aimee heard the door open behind her and was looking at June. Before Aimee could turn around she felt a hand on her shoulder, it was Kat. Aimee turned round to see Kat holding flowers, Aimee got up from the chair and hugged Kat.

Aimee said to Kat with a low voice, 'It's so hard to see her like this she's always so full of life.'

'I know,' Kat replied putting her arm around Aimee and they leaned on each other with their heads tilted towards each other. Kat added, 'Don't worry soon she will be up and about dancing again.'

Aimee smiled, Kat looked at an unconscious June and said to her, 'You always had time for me June, get well soon.' Kat then turned to Aimee and said, 'I remember that time we were at her place and I was moody because Josh had dumped me, and June said "Kat there's no fella worth crying over."' There was a pause and then Kat added, 'I miss her cakes, she bakes the best cakes,' Aimee and Kat continued to talked to each other for several minutes.

Around the same time, Matt had arrived at the hospital. Emma met Matt at ground floor reception, 'Thank you for coming Matt, it would mean so much to Aimee,' Emma said. Emma had asked Matt to come to the hospital and support Aimee, Emma walked with him to the intensive care unit

on the 1st floor, she opened the door to the ward and Matt was stood behind Emma. Kat and Aimee turned round as they heard the door open, Emma then said, 'Oh Kat it's so good of you to come,' Kat and Matt then saw each other - they did not greet each other. Matt walked up to Aimee and gave her a hug, Kat avoided eye contact with Matt.

'I will get us all something to drink,' Emma said and left the room. Aimee felt uncomfortable with her best friend and boyfriend in the same room with so much resentment towards each other.

Matt did not know Kat would be at the hospital and Aimee did not know Matt was invited to the hospital.

Several hours had passed since the evening, it was now 1.45am. Matt, Kat, Aimee, Emma, Jerome, and Tom were still in the hospital, all of them in the waiting room near intensive care. Kat was tired and sleepy and for a second closed her eyes, her head dropped slightly, Emma walked up to Kat and put her hand on Kat's shoulder, Emma said to Kat, 'Why don't you head home and get some rest sweetheart, do you want Jerome to give you a lift?'

Kat replied, 'No I can get a taxi.'

'Ok' said Emma and Kat hugged her firmly. She then embraced Aimee before she left the hospital.

It was 1.54am, suddenly the ECG machine monitoring June raised an alarm indicating something was wrong; the intensive care staff rushed into the ward with a sense of urgency. Emma, Aimee, Tom and Jerome were standing watching with concern. Matt was sat down and was looking at the floor, Emma was asking the nurses what was happening, June had flat lined.

The family were asked to leave the ward and go to a waiting room. Whilst in the waiting room Emma was held closely by Jerome as Matt tried to take Aimee by the hand, but she pulled away. Aimee was biting the inside of her lip and Emma was crying.

Eleven minutes later a doctor came into

the room with a motionless look on their face. Once Emma saw the look on the doctor's face her heart sunk. 'Emma I'm very sorry we did all we can but June passed away,' said the doctor. In that moment Emma let out a loud wail and Jerome, Aimee and Tom surrounded Emma and held her. Aimee was in tears; Jerome took a deep breath and shuddered, Matt simply stood in the corner of the waiting room and he put his hand on his head.

It was 8.13am in the morning, a few hours earlier the Larkson household had arrived back home; Jerome drove back from the hospital with Tom, Emma, and Aimee as passengers. All the family were at home, on Emma's mind was making plans for the funeral. She was in the kitchen in her pyjamas staring at the floor, reflecting on the last time she saw her mum, the last time she held her. Jerome came into the kitchen, Emma had not noticed him. He put his hand on her back to comfort her, she turned around and they embraced.

Aimee was upstairs in her bedroom, she sat on her bed in her pyjamas, numbly looking at pictures on her phone of her and June; the times they spent at concerts, at the theatre, on holiday, celebrating birthdays. Aimee was scrolling through all the pictures she could find of herself and June and a tear fell from her eye onto the phone screen. She whispered, 'I love you Nan, I'm sorry.' The guilt Aimee was feeling was because she could have spent more time with June but instead, she had prioritised time with Matt.

Jerome came upstairs to see Aimee. He walked into her bedroom, sat on the bedside and hugged her, 'Do you want breakfast?' he asked Aimee. 'Let me make you something,' he added.

'I don't want to eat,' she responded and there was a pause. Jerome nodded and put his hand on Aimee's knee, he then left her bedroom.

Later that day, Friday afternoon, Kat came to see Aimee. She knocked at the front door of the Larkson house and Emma opened the front door. Kat and Emma looked at each other for a few seconds without saying anything and then they hugged and held each other for a minute. Even though they were not related, Kat could feel Emma's pain. Emma took a deep breath, 'Aimee is upstairs,' Emma said to Kat.

Kat went upstairs to Aimee's bedroom and opened the bedroom door; Aimee got up from the bed and embraced Kat and Kat kissed Aimee on the cheek. They both put their arms around each other, Aimee resting her forehead on Kat's shoulder, 'I am not going to pretend to know what you are going through,' Kat said to her best friend, then both of them sat on the side of the bed.

They held each other's hands, Aimee shook her head and said, 'I thought I would see her again, that we would speak to each other again, but I kept putting it off.'

'No one knows the future,' Kat replied,

'I feel like I let her down,' said Aimee, and

she took a deep breath.

'No you didn't, she loved you so much, Aimz' Kat replied, there was a pause.

'Have you eaten? Kat asked, there was no response from Aimee. Aimee had a blank look and was staring at the carpeted bedroom floor.

Kat said to Aimee, 'You should have something to eat,' Kat reached into her tote bag and brought out a pack of muffins, opened the pack and gave a blueberry muffin to Aimee, which Aimee started to eat hungrily. She took a few bites and Kat placed the remaining three muffins on the bedside table.

Aimee put her head on the pillow and laid back in bed, with her head and body facing sideward as Kat laid in bed taking position behind Aimee. She put her hand on Aimee's waist and rested her chin on Aimee's neck. There was quiet in the bedroom and neither Kat nor Aimee spoke. Around twenty minutes later Aimee fell asleep; she hadn't slept since coming home from college the day before.

Several hours had passed and it was now the evening around 8.49pm and Emma was in the bathroom running a bath. As the bath started to fill up Emma took her clothes off and slowly lowered into the bathtub, taking a deep breath as she felt the warm water against her skin.

She leaned her head back, resting against the bathroom tiles, and all she could feel was grief, her emotions led to her crying quietly in the bath. The house was quiet and at the same time Aimee was upstairs walking past the bathroom door, she thought she heard her mum crying. Aimee leaned her ear to the door, 'Mum are you ok?' she asked and there was no response from Emma.

Emma leaned forward in the bath and put her hand over her mouth with her eyes closed, she sniffed and opened her eyes, 'I am ok,' she said responding to Aimee, who moved away from the bathroom door and went back to her bedroom.

Twelve minutes later Emma came out of

the bathroom and she put on her pyjamas and went into her daughter's bedroom.

Aimee was sat at her desk in the bedroom and Emma walked up to her. They looked at each other with a sad expression and hugged each other.

'I miss her so much,' Aimee said and Emma took her hand.

Emma replied, 'When I had you, when you were born, June said to me that you were the most beautiful girl she had ever seen.' Aimee smiled, 'She told me that I should let you be whoever you want to be,' Emma added. 'She loved you and your brother so much.' Emma sat at the foot of the bed facing Aimee and for another hour they remembered and talked about June, eventually saying goodnight to each other.

A few days later the time came for June's funeral, attended by Emma, Jerome, Aimee, Tom, Kat, Leyton, June's older brother and uncle to Emma, as well as several of June's friends.

It was the last weekend in February, on a Sunday morning at 11.54 am and Aimee met up with her driving instructor for her weekend driving lesson. She met him as usual on a small quiet road in Reigate, about a three-minute walk from her house. Looking up to check the weather she saw grey skies.

Aimee walked up to the white Ford Fiesta, which was a dual controlled car, parked at the side of the street and her driving instructor opened the driver door and stepped out of the car. 'Hi John, good morning,' Aimee said to him.

'Aimee how are you doing today?' John replied cheerfully.

'Ok thanks,' said Aimee; John was standing by the driver's side of the car.

'Do you want to come over here and take a seat on the driver side?'

'Sure,' Aimee responded and they both got into the car together, John sitting on the passenger side at the front and Aimee sitting in the driver's seat.

John was 5 foot 9 with balding grey hair and he was wearing a light blue shirt with a navy-blue jumper over it, topped by a classic tweed jacket. Aimee was wearing a black, short sleeve top with a blue denim jacket over it, blue denim skirt and white trainers. John said to Aimee, 'Have you adjusted your seat, is it ok?'

'Yes that is fine.'

'Mirrors look fine?' John asked

Aimee responded, 'Yes.'

'Did you have a good week, Aimee?' he asked smiling, 'What did you get up to?'

'No this week wasn't great,' said Aimee looking at the windscreen.

'Oh dear sorry to hear that,' John replied looking at Aimee, 'Hope everything is ok with your friends.' he added.

Aimee nodded, waiting for her instructor to give an idea of today's driving lesson, John put his hands together and looked at Aimee and raised both eyebrows, 'Well if you ever want to talk about it anytime, just let me know,' he said to her.

'Thanks,' Aimee replied politely.

'I think you will find I'm a very good listener,' he said smiling. 'Right, let's get started. I will give you directions,' John added. Aimee put the car key into the ignition to turn on the engine, released the handbrake and put the car in gear to drive, signalling and checking her mirrors as she drove off.

As they were driving John said to Aimee, 'Right your test centre will be Redhill Aerodrome, so in future lessons we will learn some routes around there but today we will try some new routes, just follow the signs and we will be heading to Epsom.'

Aimee stopped the car at a red light near Reigate Hill, her instructor briefly looked down at her knee. Aimee could sense John was staring so she looked back at him and John gave a wry smile, 'Carry on the light is green," he said to Aimee as the traffic lights turned green. Aimee was driving on a major road with the speed limit of 30 miles per hour and there was a car driving behind Aimee. She looked to her right and there was a minor road with traffic joining the major road, she meant to continue driving, however a car coming from her right and from the minor road was heading onto the major road so, for this reason, Aimee hesitated and slowed down as the other driver joining the main road was speeding. John said, 'What are you doing? You go, you have priority you don't have to stop.'

Aimee replied, 'Yes but I wanted to...'

'You have right of way,' John interrupted,

Aimee said to him, 'I wanted to make sure because they were approaching fast,' John ignored her and didn't reply.

A few minutes later whilst driving, they were at a dual carriageway and Aimee signalled to move to the left lane and drove the car into the left lane. When John saw this he said to Aimee, 'Always check your mirrors before you switch lane, remember *mirror signal manoeuvre*, we talked about this before.'

'I did,' she replied,

'Not properly' John replied, Aimee was a little annoyed with the comment, they were now approaching a larger roundabout with 3 lanes and 4 exits, the traffic was heavy, the Ford Fiesta Aimee was driving was in the 3rd lane. Aimee was getting ready to drive into the roundabout and could see cars constantly approaching into the roundabout from her right. The roundabout had no traffic lights, so decision making was based on time, space, and anticipation.

With the build-up of traffic behind her and the pace at which the cars from the right were entering the roundabout, it made Aimee feel apprehensive and nervous.

'You could have gone then,' John her instructor said to her, implying that Aimee could have moved the car into the roundabout. Aimee then heard a car's horn but could not identify which car it was or which lane the horn came from.

The palms of Aimee's hands were sweaty and she felt a rush of blood to her head, a heat that came over her. As she tried to move the car into the roundabout, the car in front broke abruptly and Aimee, instead of braking, had put her foot on the accelerator and the Ford Fiesta car she was driving was inches away from hitting the car in front, suddenly in that split second Aimee had a flash back of a car accident years ago. A car accident with her and her dad, in which her dad lost his life, and in that moment an overwhelming sense of fear and then grief flooded Aimee and she was distraught. In shock, she froze, and the car stalled.

John reacted quickly, 'What are you doing?' he said to Aimee; John used the mirrors to look at the traffic around, Aimee looked down at the steering wheel she was in shock and upset.

'It's ok I can still drive,' she said, and attempted to change gears and start the car. John told her to stop but Aimee continued struggling with the gearbox.

'Just stop!' John said and he put the car's hazard lights on, got out of the car, made a quick gesture to apologise to the drivers behind them and walked in front of the car moving to the driver's side.

Aimee quickly got out of the driver's seat and walking around the car she sat in the front passenger seat, her head in her hands. John turned off the hazard lights and started driving. Around six minutes later he found a street to park in and parked the car in a safe place. Aimee was leaning her head against the car window on the front passenger side, her face expressionless. All she could think of was seeing the body of her dad in pain; her memories of the life leaving her dad's body as he was trapped in the car, the near miss she had just had it had all triggered memories of the car accident with her dad.

John said to Aimee, 'What was that?'

'I am sorry,' she responded, 'you won't understand, I just want to go home,'

Aimee added sniffing.

John said to her, 'Look its ok,' he then put his left hand on her knee.

'What are you doing?' Aimee said surprised, she quickly moved her knee.

'I was just making sure you are ok Aimee,' John responded with a puzzled look as Aimee opened the passenger door and stepped out of the car. She walked away with her arms crossed and John also stepped out of the car and shouted to Aimee, 'We still have one hour of the lesson left!' John shook his head as he walked away from the car to follow Aimee.

She said to him, 'Please leave me alone,' as she stood on the street pavement. Aimee walked to a nearby street where she found a bench. She sat down and took a deep breath, holding her head in her hands and holding back the tears as the memories of losing her father overwhelmed her. She stayed there for a few minutes before she decided to walk home.

At 2.41pm that afternoon Aimee

discussed the car incident with her mum, she lay on her bed with her mum by the bedside, Aimee said to Emma, 'It was fine, I was driving and then when we got to the roundabout, seeing all the cars took me back there to that moment, I don't know what happened, I just froze as it all came back to me, everything that happened in the accident!'

Emma nodded, 'It's ok, you went through a lot that day; we all miss him and when you are ready, you can have your driving lessons with Jerome, or with me, or just take a break it's up to you sweetheart.' Emma paused and then added, 'I know you still remember the accident and I want you to also know of the good times. You know your father was the kindest man; when he found out I was pregnant with you he was on his knees crying tears of joy - we were both crying. When I got the call about the accident, I just remember thinking *God I don't want to lose both of you*,' Emma took a deep breath. 'He wanted the best for you. When you were born he was calm, and then you came out and the first time he held you he burst out crying.' Emma said and they both smiled as they reflected. Aimee then sat up and hugged her mum.

In the evening, John her driving instructor sent Aimee a text message. *Sorry about that, hope you are feeling better now, would be good to continue lessons.*

Aimee didn't respond.

MARCH

It was a weekday afternoon at Aston Gate College, at lunchtime Aimee and Matt were sat in the 6th form common room next to each other on a sofa and Aimee put her hand on Matt's thigh.

  Leyton and other 6th formers were sat opposite and around Matt and Aimee. There were two 4-seater sofa's opposite each other, and a single chair to the left and right of the sofas. The guys were in conversation about football. Aimee looked up to the entrance door of the common room and she then saw Lucy coming into the common room smiling, carrying her handbag by her side. Aimee couldn't take her eyes off Lucy. although they had never spoken to each other, Aimee always noticed Lucy from afar and thought Lucy was beautiful but also interesting.

Lucy was wearing a floral print swing mini dress with short sleeves, and recently changed her hair from brunette to blonde with a wavy cut and curtain bangs. Lucy walked to the sofa and then sat next to Leyton, Lucy looked at Leyton smiling, Leyton smiled in response, Lucy relaxed her hand on his thigh, Aimee was a little confused watching their body language as Lucy proceeded to kiss Leyton on the mouth then flicked her hair back. Leyton leaned in again to kiss her on the cheek, they continued to hold hands as they sat down, Lucy gently put her hand behind Leyton's head stroking his hair softly. In that moment Aimee's heart sunk, she could feel heat over her head and chest, surprised at what she was seeing, not knowing where to look. Aimee looked away to other students in the common room, pretending not to care or notice the affection between Leyton and Lucy, it was so difficult for her to understand this was happening, she had no idea Leyton and Lucy were an item, she bit the inside of her lip and looked to the floor.

Leyton could see that Aimee's gaze was fixed to the floor, 'Aimee you ok?' he asked, she raised her head and nodded. Matt had no reaction, just a disinterested gaze towards Leyton. Lucy, Leyton, Matt and friends continued to talk in the common room.

Aimee felt sick, she got up and decided to go to the toilet, she left the common room and went into the lady's toilet, went into a vacant cubicle and put down the lid of the toilet seat. Aimee sat on the seat and gave out a huge sigh, she placed her hand on her head and pulled back her hair, moments later as Aimee came out of the cubicle, she saw Lucy at the mirrors. Lucy could see Aimee's reflection and saw Aimee coming out of the cubicle, Aimee quickly broke eye contact and moved forward to wash her hands, Lucy was quiet as she was checking her make up in the mirror. Feeling awkward Aimee just wanted to leave, 'See you around,' Lucy said to Aimee with a slight smile and proceeded to leave the toilets.

Aimee went out of the toilets and instead of going back to the 6th form common room, she went outside of the college building to be alone, She went to the side entrance of the building, there she saw Leyton standing by himself, 'Oh hi,' Aimee said to Leyton and Leyton gave a little wave, there was an awkward silence as they stood next to each other. 'I haven't seen you in a while, hope you are doing well,' Aimee said moving closer to Leyton with her hands clasped together, 'I've missed you,' she added.

Leyton smiled and said, 'Thanks, all good,' and there was a pause, 'Sorry, should have told you about....'

Before he could finish, Aimee said to him, 'That's ok none of my business, but it would be good to.......' before Aimee could say more, the doors of the side entrance opened, Lucy walked through them. Lucy then walked towards Leyton who turned round to see her, they kissed and Lucy put her arms around Leyton's waist and told him to come inside, Lucy took Leyton by the hand and they walked to the side entrance door, as they walked away Lucy looked over her shoulder back at Aimee.

APRIL

A few days later, it was the weekend, a Saturday afternoon. Kat went to the Larkson house to meet Emma. Kat knew Aimee would not be at the house during the afternoon, as Aimee recently got a job in retail and now works every Saturday afternoon in a supermarket. Kat wanted to speak to Emma privately in-person. Kat approached the front door of 49 Faircroft Road, Emma was in the hallway and could see through the frosted glass that someone was standing at the door. Emma was in her navy-blue Egyptian cotton dressing gown, she was barefoot, she opened the door and saw Kat standing at the door. Kat was wearing a basic beanie, black knitted roll neck jumper and grey jeans, Emma said to Kat, 'Oh hi Kat Aimee is at work now.'

'That's fine, actually I wanted to speak to you,' Kat replied.

'Oh ok come in,' said Emma and they walked into the hallway and then into the kitchen. 'Brew?' Emma asked.

'Yes please,' Kat replied, Emma opened the kitchen cupboard above the cooker where tea and coffee was stored.

'Peach and Mango, or Lemon and Ginger?' Emma asked.

'Peach and Mango please,' Kat replied.

'Sure darling,' Emma replied. Emma switched on the kettle to boil water, they then sat opposite each other at the kitchen island. 'So how are you doing?' Emma asked.

Kat nodded, 'Great,' she replied.

Emma asked, 'Are you still with what's her name, Yan?'

'No, it's Yas.' Kat replied.

'Oh sorry, Yas,' said Emma.

'We're …. Ok,' Kat said to Emma, there was a pause.

'You hesitated, what's going on?' Emma asked Kat and she put her hands on Kat's hands which were placed on the kitchen island worktop.

Kat replied, 'It's complicated with Yas, we're on and off.'

'But you like her?' Emma asked smiling. Kat smiled. 'Sorry none of my business,' Emma added. Emma released Kat's hands and got up from the bar stool opposite the kitchen island, she walked to the kettle to make tea, 'So what did you want to talk about?' Emma asked.

Kat said to Emma, 'Has Aimee mentioned anything to you about Matt?'

'What do you mean?' Emma replied.

'Anything that you were concerned about or didn't sit right with you?' Kat added.

Emma replied, 'Well, yes she has but what do you think is going on?'

'I don't think she is happy……. with Matt,'

Kat said.

Emma placed the cup of tea in front of Kat, Emma nodded slowly, Kat then said, 'My concern is,' Kat paused and sighed, leaned forward, and clasped her hands together and lowering her head, 'I feel like she is worried about standing up to him, and it's difficult for me because anytime I talk about Matt in a negative way, Aimee's mood with me changes and I don't want us to fall out because of him.'

Emma then said to Kat, 'We have talked about that, Aimee and I. She can take care of herself,' Emma added. 'In any relationship there has to be a balance, what else?' Emma asked and Kat hesitated, 'Just say it,' Emma prompted.

Kat looked Emma in the eye and then said, 'Her diet. I think Matt is telling her what to eat, or hinting at what she can't eat.'

Emma sighed and she said to Kat, 'I have noticed her eating habits changed recently, I will speak to her.'

Kat replied, 'Please don't tell her we talked

about this, it's been difficult to challenge her when it comes to addressing him.'

Emma nodded, 'Thank you for telling me, but you must give her time to make her own decisions, to learn from her decisions or mistakes,' she said. There was a pause before Emma said to Kat, 'Has your mum reached out to you Kat?' Kat took a deep breath, 'Yes, she has.' She took a sip of tea, 'But I don't know if I am ready yet,' she added.

Emma walked round and stood next to Kat, she put her arms around Kat and leaned her chin on Kat's head, 'Whenever you are ready, we are here for you,' she said to Kat. Emma added whilst holding Kat by the hand, 'Your mum knows she made terrible mistakes which she regrets, but she is ready to change, she loves you, she wants to start again, so don't hesitate to reach out to her whenever you are ready, losing June earlier this year taught me that life is too short,' Kat nodded her head. They spent another half an hour talking and then Kat left the Larkson house.

MAY

It was a Saturday afternoon, 2.13pm, Leyton was in high spirits, from his perspective his relationship with Lucy was going well, they had been dating since March. The sun was shining and the weather warm at 21 degrees. Leyton paid a visit for the first time to the Stearman household, he went to see Lucy. He walked past the pebbled driveway which had a Range Rover parked on it and approached the front door of the 4-bedroom detached house which was in Merstham, Surrey. Leyton pushed the doorbell, he was wearing a navy-blue t-shirt, beige tracksuit bottoms and black trainers. Aiden answered and opened the front door, 'Hi Mr Stearman, I am here to see Lucy,' Leyton said, there was a pause and Aiden had a confused look. 'Sorry who are you?' Aiden asked.

'Leyton Stowell, erm Lucy asked me to wait for her,' he replied.

'Oh, ok come in,' Aiden responded and they both stood in the hallway, 'Lucy didn't tell me about you,' Aiden added. Leyton smiled awkwardly, 'Come into the living room,' Aiden said to Leyton. Aiden then proceeded to sit on the sofa with his legs crossed, he took a deep breath and looked at Leyton who remained standing, 'So you're in year 12 or 13?' Aiden asked.

'Year 13, the same college as Lucy,' Leyton replied and Aiden nodded.

'And what are you studying?' he asked.

'Media, Leisure and Tourism, Geography,' said Leyton.

'Good, so what do you plan to study at University?' Aiden asked and there was a pause.

Leyton put his hands together, 'Actually I am not yet sure about Uni Mr Stearman,' he replied.

'Oh really?' Aiden said, he then sat forward.

Leyton then said, 'I am planning to do event photography,' Leyton added, 'It's great for me, I do it at the moment for clubs, parties, birthdays, weddings and I also enjoy being a DJ in my spare time, I love it,' Leyton smiled.

'So you will do that as a hobby on the side?' Aiden asked,

Leyton replied, 'No for work...... permanently.'

'So you don't have plans beyond that?' asked Aiden.

'No,' said Leyton and broke eye contact with Aiden, Leyton then cleared his throat and said, 'I don't think the 9 to 5 life is for me,' he smiled nervously. Aiden had nothing to say.

A few seconds later Lucy was just coming in, they could hear her open the front door as she put her key in and walked into the hallway, Lucy then walked into the living room, she was wearing a gym sports bra and leggings, holding a bottle of water. Oh, hi dad,' she said, her eyes moved from her dad to Leyton and there was an awkward moment of silence between Leyton, Lucy and Aiden. 'I am just going to get something from the kitchen,' said Lucy. While Lucy went to the kitchen, Leyton avoided eye contact with Aiden who was looking straight at him, unimpressed by the conversation they just had. Lucy came back into the living room, smiled briefly at her dad, she then took Leyton by the hand and moved towards the hallway.

'Nice to meet you Mr Stearman,' Leyton said as he turned away from Aiden, Aiden nodded with a brief smile, Leyton and Lucy walked upstairs together.

They went into Lucy's bedroom, 'What was that?!' Leyton said to Lucy. Lucy sniggered, she gestured to Leyton to be quiet, putting her finger on his lips and making sure her bedroom door was closed, 'Sorry that was awkward,' she said to him.

'Really?' Leyton replied sarcastically, Lucy took Leyton by the hand, and they were now both standing by the bed, Leyton took his t-shirt off quickly and they began to kiss, they both then took off their trainers.

Lucy put her arms around Leyton's neck, Leyton then sat on the side of the bed and Lucy sat on his lap facing him, she wrapped her legs around his waist and they continued to kiss. Lucy then got up and took her gym wear off and laid with her back on the bed, Leyton proceeded to kiss Lucy on her neck as he lay on top of her, he slowly kissed every part of her neck, Lucy began to breathe slowly, her mouth open, both their hands clutched tightly together, Leyton bringing forward his tongue and moving it up and down Lucy's neck slowly, Lucy moved on the bed putting her naked back towards Leyton and lay on her belly, he started to kiss her back, moving up from the bottom of her spine to the back of her neck.

As they continued to kiss, they faced each

other lying side by side on the bed, she put her finger on his lips, moving her finger to feel the shape of his lips, at that precise moment Lucy's mobile phone vibrated on the bedside table due to a WhatsApp message received, the message was from Matt *what are u up to?* Lucy ignored her phone and hadn't read the message. Leyton covered himself and Lucy with the duvet, Lucy was on her back resting her head on the pillow, Leyton moved down the bed and placed his head between Lucy's thighs, he then began to kiss her inner thigh, pushing his lips against the skin of her thigh, moving from the right to left thigh, he then slowly pulled down Lucy's underwear, he placed his lips below and began to go down on her. Lucy placed her hand on Leyton's head and her other hand she used to cover her mouth, she was trying not to make a loud sound even whilst receiving intense pleasure.

It was three hours later and Leyton was ready to leave, Lucy came downstairs with him before saying goodbye. As Leyton walked past the living room, he politely said goodbye to Aiden; Aiden nodded but said nothing to Leyton. Lucy kissed Leyton and closed the front door. As she walked upstairs Aiden wanted to say something, but he decided to read a book and sat in the living room.

A few more hours had passed and in the evening, Lucy came downstairs for a cup of water, she was wearing her pyjamas. She went to the kitchen and poured herself a glass of water. As she came out of the kitchen she intended to head to the stairs, to go to her bedroom. Aiden called her from the living room, 'Lucy!' he said, she rolled her eyes and sighed whilst standing by the door of the living room. Aiden hadn't seen Lucy's reactions, Lucy walked into the living room holding the glass of water and sat down opposite her dad, there was a pause, Aiden put down the book he was reading and said to Lucy, 'You didn't tell me about Leyton, it would have been good to know about him before I met him, I was not impressed.' Aiden sighed, 'This Leyton, what is going on there?' he asked.

'What do you mean? I ...... like him' Lucy replied.

'Ok tell me, does he have any short or long term goals?' Aiden asked his daughter.

'He is into photography, he enjoys it' Lucy replied. There was a pause.

'Do you know his friends, do you trust his friends?' Aiden asked.

'I don't know all his friends, but he gets on well with everyone at college,' said Lucy. Aiden had previously taken a look at Leyton's Instagram profile, he put his phone on the table in front of Lucy, on the screen of the mobile phone was a picture from Leyton's Instagram account.

Lucy said to her dad, 'Yes I have seen this.'

'So these pictures with other girls you are happy with that and the obscene gestures he is making?' asked Aiden.

'He takes pictures for club nights to make extra money,' she replied to her dad.

'Pictures of smoking and the language he uses!' said Aiden.

Lucy pulled in and closed her lips, she then asked, 'Why don't you just say what the real problem is?'

'Don't go down that path with me,' Aiden said sternly, his eyes widening in annoyance. 'I will put an end to this if you don't!' he added. Aiden sat back and regained his composure, he said to his daughter, 'You are at an important stage in your life and this is not the first time I have said this to you, if he is not going to help you move forward, help you grow intellectually, then he will pull you back. I will not stand by and pretend I can ignore this joke of a relationship, are we clear?' Lucy felt a rush of blood to her face, she looked down at her glass of water and could not make eye contact with her dad, she put down the glass of water on the table, got up from the sofa quickly and went to her bedroom, she closed the door, turned off the lights and put herself under the duvet and started to cry quietly.

The following Saturday afternoon around

2.50pm, Leyton's parents had organised a barbeque for friends and family at their home in Merstham Surrey. Leyton had asked Lucy to join him, She didn't think it was a good idea, but eventually he persuaded her. Leyton was optimistic about the prospect of introducing Lucy to his family and friends.

Lucy approached the terraced house where Leyton lived, she came through the open front door, she went through the hallway into the kitchen. As she approached the entrance to the kitchen, she looked above the door and there was a small Jamaican flag. Lucy looked ahead and saw Leyton's mum standing in the kitchen, Leyton's mum smiled at her, 'Hello sweetheart,' she said moving closer.

'Yes hi,' Lucy replied with a wave, Leyton's mum Esther took Lucy by the hand and hugged her, Esther said to Lucy, 'Welcome, it's good to see you again,' Esther beamed with a smile as she was very fond of Lucy. 'Go through to the garden dear, Leyton is there,' Esther said to Lucy. 'Would you like something to drink?' she asked Lucy.

'I'm ok thanks,' leaving the kitchen Lucy went to the garden. As she came into the garden she could smell roasted meat, the light and heat of the sun hit her face, she raised her hand to shield her face, there were about eleven other people in the garden, Leyton turned around and saw Lucy, he smiled, approached her to give her a drink and leaned forward to kiss her. She didn't reciprocate so he kissed her on the cheek.

'Thanks for coming, are you ok you?' Leyton said to Lucy, 'You haven't called me recently, I like talking to you every day,' he added smiling.

Lucy said to him, 'Sorry just a few things on my mind', Leyton put his hand on Lucy's shoulder, 'Well exams are over now and I'm sure you did great,' he said to her, Lucy gave a weak smile.

Leyton said, 'My cousin is coming over soon, but let me introduce you to my....'

Lucy interrupted him holding him by the

arm, she looked him in the eye, 'Leyton,' she said, there was a short pause, 'I don't think we should see each other again,' she added.

Leyton smiled then lowered his smile, 'What?' he responded.

'It's just better for the longer term trust me.'

'When did you decide this?' he put down his drink on the table in the garden. 'If you are having doubts and you need some time that's fine, we can take it easy,' he said to Lucy. He faced her and held both her hands, she couldn't look at him and bit her lip taking a step back from him.

Lucy said, 'What do you want me to do, pretend everything is ok?' she was holding back her emotions but devastated.

Leyton paused to reflect, he looked at her and shook his head, then after a pause he sighed, 'Your dad doesn't like me.'

Lucy closed her eyes and shook her head, 'He's protective, I don't think he is going to change his mind,' she said looking down to the grass with her arms crossed.

Leyton sniggered and looked to the sky, he then said to Lucy, 'When I invited you here this is not what I had in mind.'

'I told you I didn't want to come,' Lucy said with a low voice, Leyton's uncle approached them smiling, he then looked up and down at Lucy, 'Leyton are you going to introduce me to your beautiful friend?'

'Uncle this is Lucy,' Leyton's uncle brought forward his hand towards Lucy, Lucy gave him a weak handshake.

The uncle put his hand on Leyton's shoulder, 'Talk to you in a bit, you have done very well there,' he said to Leyton, smiling and leaning into his ear and then walked away.

Lucy said to Leyton, 'I'm sorry, I really want us to still stay close,' she held him by the hand as she wiped a tear from her eye, Leyton withdrew and stepped back.

'I am going to go,' she said, her voice was breaking, and Lucy left, walking away

TOBI TAIWO

from the garden.

As Lucy left the garden she came into the kitchen, walking past Leyton's mum who noticed her, Esther said to Lucy, 'Hope you're having a good time love.'

Lucy smiled but with tears rolling down her cheek, she said to Esther, 'I'm sorry, thank you but I have to go,' Esther had a confused look as she watched Lucy rush to the front door and leave the house.

Leyton turned to the garden fence with his back to the party guests, he did not want anyone to see him as he was holding back the tears. his mother Esther put her hand on her sons back and said to him with a soft voice, 'I know,' as she had observed the interaction between her son and Lucy earlier. He took in a deep breath, she held his hand, 'You just keep smiling for our guests and everything will be alright, we can talk about it later,' she said to Leyton. 'I want you to enjoy today,' she added. Esther turned around to the other guests in the garden and smiled, to give the impression that all was ok.

An hour later Kat came to see Leyton, she walked into the house and saw him in the living room, Kat and Leyton hugged. Leyton's morale was low; he sat on the living room sofa looking down at the floor. They sat next to each other on the sofa, Kat asked Leyton, 'What happened?'

Leyton replied, 'Her dad, I know he's never liked me anyway, what surprised me is just how she did it, how she just disconnected,' Kat took her friend's hand.

'Just focus on yourself, don't let this change you,' she said, 'Keep focussing on your passion and the next person that comes along will notice your energy mate,' she added.

Kat added, 'For now I know you will be upset for a while, and anything you see that reminds you of Lucy could be upsetting, but if you ever want to talk, I'm here. And please don't think she hates you; this would have upset her as well.'

Kat got up from the sofa, she smiled at Leyton, 'Let's go to the garden and show everyone how to party,' she said.

It was around 7.02pm in the evening, Leyton's mum and sister were in the kitchen talking to Kat, 'Congrats on the engagement,' Kat said to Leyton's older sister Karis.

'Thanks,' replied Karis with a smile. Karis turned to her brother Leyton and asked, 'Where is Lucy?' there was a pause.

'We broke up.'

'Oh,' she then turned to Kat and asked, 'Where is Aimee, I haven't seen her in a while?'

'She is working this weekend,' Kat responded.

'Hopefully both of you can make it to my wedding next month.'

'I would love to be there Karis,' Kat smiled putting her hand behind Karis back.

'Kat if you need a lift home later just let me know,' Karis said to her as she hugged Kat. Karis left the kitchen to head to the garden and continued to party with the rest of the guests.

Leyton took Kat by the hand to his bedroom, she followed him upstairs, as they went upstairs, they could hear "Family Affair" by Mary J Blige blasting as music from the garden.

Kat and Leyton sat down on the bed, Kat was holding a beer in one hand and her other hand was on Leyton's thigh, 'How are things going with Yas?' Leyton asked Kat, Kat looked down and smiled, then she looked him in the eye and continued smiling, 'Good then I take it?' said Leyton. 'I have seen the way you are together, its intense.' he added.

Kat said to Leyton, 'She's fun, she's interesting, she has so much energy and mate ………. she's a really great kisser too,' as she said this, she was touching her neck.

'Oh!' said Leyton in excitement for his friend, 'I'm happy for you, both of you couldn't keep your hands off each other when you met at Lewis's birthday.' he added.

'Anyway, let's take a picture for Aimee,

she's missing the fun,' Kat suggested to Leyton; they sent the selfie to Aimee on WhatsApp and continued talking in the bedroom for another hour. Kat took Leyton by the hand, leaving the bedroom heading back to the garden, and they danced for the rest of the night. At the end of the night when most of the guests had left, Leyton got to his bedroom, he leaned against the door and gave a huge sigh, he took out his mobile phone and deleted all the pictures on his phone of him and Lucy and all the messages they had sent each other.

Two days later, Monday morning 11.56am, Matt and Lewis were revising, they were in the library of Aston Gate College, which was on the second floor of the building. They sat opposite each other on blue cushioned chairs. There was a white modern rectangular table in front of them. To the left of Matt, which was the right of Lewis was a huge glass panel which was floor to ceiling in height and across the whole floor of the library, it gave a great view of Reigate Surrey, the sun light came through the glass panel shining on to the carpeted floor of the library.

The library was not busy and there were only a few students around Matt and Lewis. Matt was wearing a white regular fit short sleeve shirt with light blue skinny jeans; Lewis was wearing a navy-blue short sleeve polo shirt with beige chinos. On the table in front of them were text books, an energy drink, pens, highlighters and revision notes.

'Right, time for a break.' said Lewis. Matt and Lewis got up from their seats and headed for the library exit.

Matt and Lewis left the library, they went through the entrance of the library. In front of the library doors there was a staircase. On the right, were stairs leading up to the third floor, on the left were stairs leading down to the first floor. They started walking down the stairs, they got to the level of the first floor and wanted to walk further down the staircase to the ground floor, at this time Kat was walking up the staircase, she was heading to the library.

Kat was holding text books as she walked, she was wearing a dusty pink roll sleeve button front blouse and short denim skirt. She saw Lewis and Matt coming towards her on the stairs, they looked at Kat and Kat looked at them as they passed each other. Lewis said openly 'Careful, she might try to push you,' he was jokingly referring to Kat pushing Matt into the garden fence last year.

Kat heard this and stopped, she was at the top of the stairs, Matt and Lewis were at the bottom of the stairs, Kat said to Lewis 'Lewis you're just a dickhead, that's why Lucy dumped you, because you are a vile human being.'

'What did you say?' Lewis replied.

Lewis wanted to walk up the stairs to confront Kat, Matt quickly put his hand on Lewis's chest to hold him back. Matt looked up towards Kat and smiled sarcastically, he then said to Kat 'Didn't you like beg Aimee's family to have you over for Christmas, because you are such a loner, no one wanted to be with you,' those words hit Kat so hard, she was upset, not having her family with her for Christmas was a painful memory. Instead of showing emotion, Kat took a breath and walked away, she continued up the staircase to the library.

When Matt and Lewis left the building of Aston Gate College, Lewis said to Matt with a slight smile on his face 'Mate that was brutal.'

'She had it coming, she's been pissing me off for a while.' Matt replied.

On the same day, at 12.43pm in the afternoon, Aiden Stearman was in London. he had booked a one-bedroom suite at the Langham Hotel in London for two nights. He was standing opposite the bed in the suite in a bath robe, the sun was shining through the window and the heat of the sun's rays against the carpeted floor. Aiden looked at his phone smiling, due to the message he just received. Within moments Aiden went to the front door of the suite, he opened the door and Emma was standing at the front of the door to the suite. Emma was wearing an elegant navy-blue one shoulder thigh split maxi dress, she also had on gold hoop earrings and high heeled shoes. Aiden let Emma in and closed the door, she smiled at him and they kissed passionately. Emma held Aiden's face and locked lips with him; Aiden took Emma by her wrists and moved her wrists upwards above her head, he moved her a step back with her back against the hotel room door, they were standing opposite each other. Aiden started to kiss Emma's shoulder gently, moving to her chest and neck, he could smell her perfume, Aiden put his hand firmly on Emma's thigh through the split in her dress and she loosened his bath robe, both couldn't keep their hands of each other.

Ten minutes later they were in the king size bed together, both Emma and Aiden beneath the duvet covers. Emma was lying down with her back on the bed, she faced him and put her hands through his hair and was kissing him on his neck. Aiden moved down the bed under the duvet, kissing Emma on her chest moving down to her navel. Emma got out of the bed, nude, she got up to go to the en-suite bathroom, in the bathroom she faced the mirror.

Aiden walked up behind her, embracing her from behind and kissing her shoulders, she turned around and smiled, putting her arms around his neck, Emma had taken her phone with her to the en-suite, she left her phone on the edge of the marble bath tub, it was vibrating as Jerome was calling her. Emma was kissing Aiden, Emma saw that her mobile phone was moving on the edge of the bath, she tried to get it but Aiden stopped her, he carried Emma and placed her on the edge of the marble bathroom sink, she was in a sitting position, 'It's cold' she said laughing, Emma could feel the cold surface of the marble sink, Aiden kneeled down and started to kiss the inside of Emma's thighs, Emma leaned back slightly as Aiden placed his face between her thighs, Aiden pushing his lips further forward and using his tongue, Emma moaned in pleasure with her mouth open. Jerome was calling her again, 'Leave it,' said Aiden and he continued to go down on Emma.

'No I have to pick up he is going to worry,' Emma said. Aiden sighed, he got up and went to the suite, Emma answered her phone.

Emma answered, 'Hey you ok?'

Jerome said, 'Just on my lunch break, was checking when you will be home this evening.'

'Erm the conference will finish around 5.30 but the team might be out for drinks after'.

'Ok, don't stay out too late or you will miss the train, we will see you later then'.

'Love you, bye'.

'Bye,' Jerome ended the call.

Emma sighed, she also felt slight guilt

for lying to Jerome. Aiden opened the bathroom door and presented a luxury lingerie gift set to Emma. He said to her, 'You can wear it next time you see me.'

Emma smiled and replied, 'I can't accept this!'

'I can already picture you in it.'

'You are the worst,' she said to him.

'That's what you love about me,' Aiden replied, they started kissing.

'I have so much on, and I need to think about keeping the family together,' Emma said.

'Aimee and Tom are grown up,' replied Aiden, 'Focus on your happiness,' he added.

Aiden and Emma spent a few more hours together enjoying each other's company, flirting, kissing, making love. Emma left to go home back to Reigate late in the evening.

It was Thursday evening 7.09pm, Jerome

and Emma were sat together in the living room on the sofa, watching television. Jerome had his hand over the back of the sofa and Emma's mobile phone was vibrating as a call came in. She ignored the call, her mobile phone rang again vibrating in her pocket and Emma ignored it. Jerome sat forward on the sofa and sighed heavily with his hands clasped, 'What?' Emma asked looking at him, Jerome picked up the remote control on the coffee table and muted the television, 'Do you want to get that?' he said looking at Emma sternly.

'No, it's ok'

'Who is it then?'

Emma just shook her head, 'Give me your phone.' Jerome said calmly.

'For what?' said Emma.

'I am here Emma!!' Jerome shouted.

Aimee heard the noise from upstairs in her bedroom and put her headphones on to listen to music.

Jerome shouted, 'I am present in this

relationship, what the hell is going on!?' Emma crossed her arms and crossed her legs, Jerome got up from the sofa and he turned to her and said, 'You think I don't notice you sneak to the toilet or garden with your phone?' he added, 'You come home late from God knows where!'

Emma sighed looking at Jerome with a motionless face, she put her hands on her hair and pulled back her hair, 'Listen to yourself,' she replied, 'You sound absurd, are you done?' she said to Jerome.

Jerome replied, 'Whatever this is, you need to stop and take a hard look at yourself in the mirror.'

Emma got up and faced Jerome, 'Don't raise your voice at me!'

'It's you that needs to give more Emma, I've got nothing to hide, but you keep treating me with contempt,' he said. Jerome, frustrated, walked away, and slammed the living room door.

A day later, Friday evening at 6.44pm

Jerome had returned from work, he parked the car in the driveway, put his house key into the lock, opened the front door and came upstairs, meeting Emma in the bedroom. She was standing opposite the free-standing bedroom mirror, wearing a white bodycon backless dress and putting her gold earrings on. He walked up behind her and could smell her perfume, Jerome put his arms around her waist, moved his head forward slowly to give her a kiss, she turned her cheek away. 'I'm out with the girls tonight, don't stay up for me,' Emma said to Jerome, he started to give her a kiss on the neck. 'I have to go' Emma said to him.

'Stay,' he said, whispering in her ear, he then sighed and sat on the edge of the bed. 'Ok so where are you meeting up?' he asked Emma.

'We haven't decided yet, I will probably go to Nicola's house,' said Emma. She then kissed Jerome on the cheek and closed the bedroom door and went downstairs. Jerome was beginning to get suspicious as he sat on the bedside. He got up and watched Emma from the bedroom window as she left the house, Emma got into a taxi which was outside the house.

Jerome went downstairs, Aimee shouted at him from the living room, 'What do you want for dinner?'

'Nothing thanks,' replied Jerome as he rushed to his car. Jerome then waited a few seconds and pulled out of the driveway, following the taxi that picked up Emma. The taxi stopped and parked seven minutes later, on a street in Merstham, Surrey. Jerome parked his car on the same street, he lowered his head so he wouldn't be seen by Emma. He saw Emma come out of the taxi and walk to the front door of a house, holding a bottle of wine, Emma flicked her hair and looked around to see if anyone noticed her.

Aiden opened the front door bringing his head forward slightly into the open, they kissed briefly. When Jerome saw this from the car, his heart sunk, he felt disgusted and closed his eyes in disbelief. He hit his head against the car horn which was on the middle of the steering wheel, the sound of the car horn was audible across the street. Aiden when he heard the car horn went to the window of the living room and looked out to the street, but he saw nothing significant. Aiden was alone in the house with Emma, his daughter Lucy and his wife were on holiday in Barcelona.

Jerome rested his head against the steering wheel, 'For fuck's sake Emma,' he whispered. Jerome was furious, he got out of the car and crossed the street. He walked to the front door of the Stearman household, raised his hand to knock on the front door, hoping to confront Aiden and Emma, but he hesitated. He pulled out his phone, he remembered Emma told him earlier that she will go to Nicola's house. Jerome had Nicola's number in his contact list, he sent her a text and asked if she was meeting Emma tonight. Nicola confirmed via text that she was not meeting up with Emma.

Jerome drove the car back to the Larkson house in Reigate and continued with the rest of his evening. Emma came back to the house at 3:21 am, she took her high heels off in the hallway. Tom, Aimee and Jerome were asleep, Emma went upstairs to the bedroom, she took her dress off and fell asleep next to Jerome straight away. Jerome heard her come into the bedroom, he waited until he could hear from Emma's breathing that she was asleep. When Emma was asleep he got out of the bed slowly, walked to Emma's side of the bed, saw her mobile phone on the bedside table. He picked it up at the same time looking at Emma to make sure she was still asleep.

Jerome tried to access Emma's mobile phone but with no success, he needed to put in a security code, he was confused because he could always access Emma's phone without restrictions before, Jerome wanted to see all the text messages, emails, calls, interactions, anything he could find between Aiden and Emma, he wanted to know how long the affair had been going on. Jerome tried to use his laptop and his phone to access Emma's Facebook, Twitter, and Instagram account but with no luck, at 5.19am he eventually went back to sleep.

Emma woke up in the morning and came downstairs to the kitchen, Jerome was cooking breakfast. She said, 'Hi,' to him whilst yawning, Jerome turned round with his arms crossed and a stern look, he took a deep breath and said to Emma.

'I am going to stay with my sister for a few weeks, it's what I need right now to clear my head.'

'Can I ask why?' Emma responded.

Jerome shook his head 'I can't even look at you,' he said in disgust. Jerome left the kitchen, went upstairs, and an hour later started packing.

A week later, on Friday in the morning, Aimee sent a WhatsApp message to Kat to find out what her plans were for the day,

Aimee: *happy Friday, what r u up to?*

Kat: *heading to Ldn*

Aimee: *of course, I remember!*

Kat: *going to see my uncle and maybe some shopping*

Aimee: *enjoy*

Kat took the 10.30am train from Reigate heading to London, the train terminated at London Victoria, she changed at London Victoria and got on the London Underground, eventually coming out of Marble Arch Station via the Central Line. It was now 11.50am and the sun was starting to shine through the clouds in London, with the pleasant weather Kat wanted to walk from Marble Arch towards Oxford Circus via Oxford Street, to explore the shops.

As she was walking past Portman Street up towards Oxford Street, she could hear the buses passing by, Kat heard someone behind her say, 'Excuse me sorry', she turned round to the person, it was a young man about 6 foot 1 in height, he was wearing frameless glasses with a black denim jacket, white t-shirt and black skinny jeans, he had a dark buzz cut hair and was clean shaven.

'HI,' Kat responded a little surprised.

He smiled and said to Kat, 'I don't usually do this, but I just saw you walk by, thought you are stunning, and wanted to say hi.'

Kat was taken aback and smiled, 'Oh ok,' she said and there was a pause.

'You seemed to be peacefully in a world of your own, nice to meet you, my name is Pierre,' he said with a hand on his chest and the other used to greet her with a handshake, they started to converse on the street, Pierre seemed to have French accent.

'Are you from London Kat?'

'No, I have come down from Surrey,' he nodded his head,

'What I noticed about you was your boots.'

'My boots?' Kat asked.

'They are really cool, stylish.'

'Thanks,' Kat was looking at him, paying attention to his smile, his eyes, the way he moved his lips, she hadn't come across a guy this confident or forward in a long time. She crossed her arms as she stood in front of him.

Pierre said to her, 'You have a unique look, your fashion sense tells me you dress for yourself not others.'

'Spot on,' Kat said with a slight smile nodding.

'Well, I have to say bye it was nice to meet you. You have forgotten my name?'

'No, I remember, it was Pierre,' Kat replied.

'Look I appreciate you are busy, but we should get a quick coffee, or a drink, I know a small pub here and you seem really interesting Kat'. Kat hesitated and Pierre added, 'just half an hour and you can get on with your day, I've got plans also to meet my friends later.'

'Ok,' said Kat, they walked towards Oxford Street for a few more minutes, 'are you from France Pierre?'

'Yes, I am only been in London for about 8 months.'

'Ok what do you do Pierre, are you studying?'

'Yes my final year in the University I study Marketing,' Kat and Pierre came to a pub *The Marlborough Head,* they walked into the pub. 'Would you like something to drink?' Pierre asked.

'A cider thanks,' Pierre also ordered a cider, they sat down indoors towards the entrance of the pub, and sat opposite each other, there was a slight smell of fried food and alcohol.

'Kat what do you want to study?'

'I am very interested in performing arts.'

'You like drama!' Pierre said with his eyebrows raised.

'No, I just like to express myself through acting.'

Kat and Pierre were still sat at the pub thirty minutes later, the conversation flowed, Pierre's French accent was heavy, but she understood all he said.

'What is the best concert you have ever been to?' Kat asked him.

'It was Coldplay in Paris, good times, and you?'

'Florence and the Machine, I have never actually been to Paris.'

'Really?! you have to come, it's beautiful,' said Pierre, he leaned forward and looked at Kat, their eyes were connected. 'I like your smile, your eyes are magnetic,' he said to her. Kat started to blush, it had been a long time since she felt this energy or attraction with a guy. Pierre pointed to cushioned seats at the back of the pub. 'It is less noisy let us move there,' he said, they moved to the back of the pub where there was a cushioned seating booth and sat next to each other.

'What is the tattoo on your neck?' he asked, 'can I see it?' Kat leaned forward, pulled aside her hair covering the back of her neck to reveal her dove tattoo,

He proceeded to show her a tattoo on his arm of an eagle, 'Why an eagle?' she asked.

'Because it flies high, it is free, powerful,' Kat nodded her head in approval, she was close enough to Pierre that she could smell his cologne. A few minutes later he placed his hand on her thigh as they were talking, Kat put her hand on his back. Pierre paused, he looked at Kat, they locked eyes and kissed slowly holding hands under the table. Kat was surprised but excited, it had been a long time since she kissed a guy, she didn't think she would have these desires again.

For a moment Kat noticed a wooden table which was facing their booth, it was about four meters away, there was a man who had been sitting at that table, following them since they came into the pub, he had a black gym bag with him which he placed on the table. Kat thought it was odd as the pub was not busy yet this stranger seemed to be watching only her and Pierre.

When Pierre saw that Kat was distracted and was looking away at the strange man, he placed his hand on her face and kissed her again. Another hour had passed, Pierre and Kat were ready to leave the pub and walked towards the doors of the pub, when they left, they stood outside on the pavement, they hugged, kissed and they exchanged numbers, Kat told him she had to leave to visit her uncle, Pierre then saw the wallpaper on Kat's phone, 'Who is that?' he asked.

'That's my best friend Aimee,' Kat said smiling,

'Hope to see you soon,' he said smiling, Pierre moved closer, and they kissed again. Kat's morale was high as she said goodbye to Pierre, she then looked for a bus to take her to Islington, where her uncle lived.

Kat arrived at her uncle's flat in Islington, he opened the front door and said to her, 'What time do you call this?'

'Sorry I'm late.'

'Ok, come in, would you like something to drink?'

'Yes, a lemonade or sprite.'

Her uncle went to the kitchen and got her a drink, her uncle was in his 40's, 6 foot 2 in height, he was wearing a t-shirt and jeans, he had black hair, his hair adjusted into a man-bun, he had a goatee beard. He came into the living room and sat on a chair opposite Kat, Kat was sat down on the sofa, the sun was shining through the window onto the wooden floor of the flat, Kat could hear the sound of children playing outside on the estate.

'Your cousin is getting married in Spain next year, it would be great if you could join us,' he said to Kat, Kat put her head down and looked to the floor.

'You two have not been speaking to each other,' he said.

'She just seems to have a different life from me and since she left London, she didn't stay in touch with me' Kat replied.

'Well, she's met someone, he's a lawyer from Madrid, a very handsome man, which brings me to you Kat.' said her uncle. He raised his eyebrows, 'No boyfriend? ...... or maybe girlfriend I don't know these days, if its girlfriend I am ok with it', he added.

'Can we stop, this is awkward,' Kat replied, they both smiled briefly.

There was a pause.

Her uncle lit a cigarette and took a deep breath.

'Ok I thought you should know; your mum will be discharged soon.'

'I don't want to talk about her.'

'I know but we have to talk about it because she misses you.'

'So that's why you wanted to see me so I can forgive her and, what, we become friends again?'

'No, I am just telling you to be ready, because she will be staying with me after she is discharged, but .... eventually she has to move back in with you in Surrey,'

Kat put her hand on her forehead, and bit the inside of her lower lip.

There was a pause.

Her uncle said to her, 'She has turned her life around Kat,'

Kat crossed her arms, 'I don't want to be in the same house as her, even in the same room with her, not after what she did.'

Her uncle leaned forward annoyed, he pointed his finger at Kat and said, 'But I can't keep paying the rent for your place and for this flat and cover your mum's bills whilst she looks for a job!'

'I know and I am trying to get a job too uncle!' Kat raised her voice.

'I'm not forcing you to get a job, what I am saying is your mother, eventually she will want to be back at her home, maybe it's good for you to live with her again.'

'She hates me.'

'No, she doesn't, if you are living with her then you can support her, stop her from falling back into a bad place, she is my sister .... and I love her. She take herself to rehab for you! Because she love you.' Kat looked at her uncle.

He added, 'Look if it gets intense living with her, then I am serious about Tenerife, you can come and stay with me in Tenerife, help me with running the bar.'

'Uncle, aren't there always fights at your bar?' Kat replied.

'Ah it's not that bad, security is better now, now ok maybe one fight a week,' he said, they both smiled.

There was a pause.

'By the way, your mum also asked about er, what is her name, Aimee, she was saying "hope she's still friends with Aimee, they care about each other, Aimee is such a nice girl", blah blah blah,' he said to Kat.

Kat smiled, 'We are still friends uncle,' she said.

She spent another hour talking with her uncle, before leaving London to go back to Reigate in Surrey.

Later in the evening, as Kat was on the Southern train from London Victoria to Reigate, Pierre sent her a WhatsApp message telling her that he was glad to meet her. Kat was pleased to see the message, she smiled whilst sat on the train, responding to Pierre that she had a good time meeting him.

The next day, Saturday, Kat was still curious about Pierre. she sent him a WhatsApp message in the afternoon, a few minutes later she could see he had read it, but he didn't respond. Pierre didn't respond for the rest of the day.

Five days later, on a Thursday evening, Kat was sat in her bed scrolling through her phone, she received a WhatsApp message from Danielle, a fellow 6th former. *Kat have you seen this?*

The message had attached to it a link to a video on YouTube. Kat sat forward on her bed, opened the YouTube video entitled, "Pierre London Pick up - Posh English Girl." She couldn't tell from the video thumbnail if she was in the video but she recognised Pierre.

The video began to play, and in shock Kat saw herself in the YouTube video, talking to Pierre on the street just as she did last Friday. She the looked at the surroundings in the video and immediately recognized that it was near Marble Arch, someone had been recording her and Pierre from a few meters away and Kat remembered what she wore that day, and it was exactly as it was in the video. As the video continued to play, Kat heard her voice in the video, she realised Pierre was wearing a hidden microphone when they met on the street. She felt betrayed, angry and exposed, her hand over her mouth, this was a 12.39 minute video. Half way through the video, Pierre was narrating saying, "ok guys you will notice I complimented her about her boots, her fashion sense, this is how to get their attention guys, when you sign up for my pick up bootcamp, I will teach you how to compliment, get their attention, pick up any girl." Kat muttered as she watched in horror, she continued to watch the video and the worst part for her was to come.

As the video continued to play, it showed Pierre and Kat kissing intimately in the pub, Kat's face and voice were clear on the video. Kat paused the video, she put her head in her hands, she felt heat over her body and her cheeks were flushed, Kat sighed.

She picked up her mobile phone and continued to play the video. Pierre was narrating, "now here I could feel her energy, the way she was looking at me, she was playing with her hair, so I go in for the kiss, guys I will teach you these skills in my bootcamp if you subscribe, teach you how to escalate, increase the sexual tension through body language." The video was now showing Kat and Pierre outside the pub as they hugged, kissed and exchanged numbers. Pierre narrated again, "Guys you can see I got her number easily. I will teach you how to step up your day game, get any girls number, so subscribe to my channel, sign up for my masterclass, where I teach you the steps to approach any woman".

Kat paused the video, she looked below the video to see it had over 62,000 views, she shook her head in disbelief, she looked to the comments section of the YouTube video, reading several comments:

she's so easy

she's not a 10 but ok well done

do you have any more clips?

she's fit

did you take her back to yours?

nice legs

you are da man

she was flirting with you

smooth daygame

she's not that pretty mate

she have insta ?

Kat thought to herself, was she the only victim? The only person Pierre has done this to? She went to the YouTube Channel surprised to find eleven other videos of

Pierre meeting other women in London and recording it; she wondered if these women knew they had been secretly filmed without consent, immediately she closed the YouTube app and tried to call Pierre but he wasn't picking up, she called Pierre again but he did not pick up and she couldn't leave a voicemail.

Kat was upset and felt exposed, powerless. She reported the video, she wasn't even sure his real name was "Pierre", she sent a text message to him, *I FOUND OUT WHAT YOU DID YOU PERV TAKE THAT VIDEO DOWN!! I AM TELLING THE POLICE*. A few hours later, Kat opened the link to the video and was relieved to see a message saying, "This video has been removed by the user", so she knew Pierre would have seen her message and she sighed in relief and fell back into her pillow. She further went on to report Pierre's YouTube channel for violation of privacy.

Kat then sent a WhatsApp message to Danielle who had initially informed Kat of the video,

Kat: *have you shown that video to anyone else, does anyone else know?*

Danielle: *no, I didn't, it came up on my YouTube feed and I told you asap*

Kat took some re-assurance from Danielle's message, but she was still apprehensive.

JUNE

Now that A level exams were coming to an end, Matt, Aimee, Kat, Leyton and Lucy had sat most of their exams. It was a sunny Saturday afternoon around 1.03pm, the weather was 24 degrees with clear blue skies, Matt was walking from his house to the bus stop, planning to take the bus from Merstham to Reigate and to meet Lucy at Reigate the town centre. He was scrolling through Lucy's Instagram profile whilst waiting for the bus, liking her posts but not commenting on them. A few minutes later the bus had arrived and took him to Reigate. Matt got off the bus and met Lucy at Reigate town centre, Lucy was wearing spliced ripped denim shorts and a yellow petite cotton crop top, she had a silver beaded belly chain around her waist, black peep toe sock boots. Matt and Lucy met outside Wagamama restaurant; they went into the restaurant which was busy with people. Lucy asked for a table for two.

Matt and Lucy were sat at the restaurant opposite each other, looking at each other. 'You have been creeping,' she said to him smiling.

'What do you mean?'

'I have like 20 notifications from you on Insta.'

'Do you have a problem with that?'

'No,' she smiled, there was a pause, 'For me, food is the best way to celebrate after exams,' Lucy added.

'Well, it is done now, end of exams.'

Lucy sat back smiling.

Matt asked her, 'Why are you so confident?'

'Well I know I did my best,' she replied whilst she looked at the food menu, 'I am going for the teriyaki vegan ramen,' she said to Matt. Whilst Matt was looking through the menu, Lucy brought out her mobile phone, she gave her phone to Matt and showed him pictures of her dad, Aiden, and Matt's dad after their 10k run.

Matt said to Lucy, 'My God he was red in the face, looks like he's going to puke.' Matt asked, 'have you started to think about University then?'

Lucy replied, 'Whatever happens will happen, right now I just want to have some fun.' She put her hand on Matt's hand which was on the table, he smiled. She looked at him inquisitively.

'What?' Matt asked and Lucy leaned over the table towards him, 'It's better when your hair is like this,' she said, with one hand she pushed his hair back holding it in place, 'Yes perfect,' Lucy added smiling.

Their food arrived, they ate and stayed in the restaurant for an hour. Matt asked for the bill, he paid and said to Lucy, 'Come lets go,' they got up and left and Matt held the restaurant door open for her. They crossed the road to get to the supermarket. Lucy was hosting a house party that Saturday evening and wanted to buy a few items, as they entered the supermarket, they could hear the checkout beep sounds from the tills and self-checkout machine. The cold air conditioning hit them at the entrance, they walked past the first aisle and Lucy was laughing at a joke that Matt made. Matt and Lucy were unaware that Aimee worked in that particular supermarket. They walked past the other aisles eventually reaching the confectionary aisle. Lucy picked up some snacks, Aimee was in the following aisle the drinks aisle and she was taking the drinks from a crate putting them unto the shelf.

As Aimee was doing this she heard and recognized Matt's voice particularly, but she could not see Matt or Lucy from the aisle she was in. She went to the end of the confectionary aisle to see if it was Matt, she then saw them from the end of the aisle. She was disappointed to see Matt with Lucy standing next to each other,

Matt laughing and Lucy smiling. She was embarrassed and angry, she did not want to be spotted by Matt or Lucy, so she wanted to leave the shop floor, and go to the staff room as she needed a moment.

As she headed to the door leading to the staff room, her team leader saw her, 'Aimee you can't leave the crates there,' he said to her. Aimee went back to the aisle, then proceeded to kneel and lower her head so she wouldn't be seen, as she continued to unpack the crates.

As Matt and Lucy were walking through the aisle Matt put his hand over Lucy's shoulder, they then left the aisle and walked towards the self-checkout machines. Although Aimee did not want to be seen she was also curious about the interaction between her boyfriend and Lucy. She still observed them from a distance.

'Aimee what are you doing? Confectionary goes into the next aisle,' said her team leader as he observed that Aimee was distracted. Aimee nodded her head in acknowledgement to her team leader but chose not to speak. When Matt heard someone calling the name "Aimee" he looked back at the aisle but saw no one there that he recognised so ignored it.

Aimee felt humiliated as she continued her shift. She struggled to concentrate and she felt betrayed, her cheeks were flushed. She had been envious in recent years of how beautiful Lucy was, which she sometimes found intimidating but to see her boyfriend with a girl prettier than her, raised her insecurity.

A few days had passed, and it was a Thursday afternoon. Matt and Aimee were together in the Larkson household, both were very pleased that their exams were over, and they could relax. Aimee did not bring up the fact she saw Matt with Lucy in the supermarket or even ask him where he was during that time, she was willing to overlook if Matt still loved her, if Matt was still affectionate towards her.

They were in Aimee's bedroom, they

started to kiss as they lay in Aimee's bed next to each other, Matt then moved to lean on top of Aimee, he was kissing her. He started to kiss her neck, he continued kissing then realised Aimee was no longer reciprocating, he looked at her and said, 'What's wrong now?'

'Sorry, there is so much going through my mind.'

'Is this a wind up?' he sighed, 'Do you know what, forget it!' Matt got up from the bed.

'Matt please,' she said to him with a sad expression. Aimee got out of the bed and walked to the other side of the bed where Matt was standing, she put her arms around his waist from behind, she said to him, 'Matt .... I just want you to hold me,' her voice was breaking, she placed her face on the back of Matt's shoulder, 'Just hold me,' she added.

Matt closed his eyes briefly and exhaled, 'This is boring,' he said, he moved her arms away to free himself, he turned round to her and faced her saying, 'You don't want to do anything fun; you're always nagging that you are worried about everything, I don't want to hear about your mum and Jerome or your exams, it's just draining.'

There was a pause.

Aimee said to him, 'Matt l want you to look at me like you love me, you don't hold me like you love me, I am not always going to be smiling or laughing, and just because I worry about what is on my mind doesn't mean I don't care about us, about you and you have not always been there for me when I needed you,' her voice broke, she moved her finger wiping a tear from her eye.

Matt moved away from Aimee and faced the bedroom window, he put his hand on his hair and pulled his hair back, 'I can't talk to you when you are like this, I am going to meet up with Lewis, I am not here to sort out your issues, there is nothing going on sexually, so what am I waiting for?' he said to her and left the bedroom. Aimee put her face in her hands and shook her head and felt abandoned by Matt, but she chose not to go after him.

Two days later, Saturday, Matt and Aimee were planning to go a house party in Redhill Surrey, the party was hosted by a fellow 6th former as they were celebrating the end of exams.

The plan was for Aimee to meet Matt at his parents' house first before they went to the party.

It was 7.36pm in the evening, Aimee knocked on the front door, Lorraine was in and she answered, opening the front door for Aimee to come through into the hallway, she embraced Aimee warmly, 'You look absolutely stunning Aimee,' Lorraine said, she stepped back and smiled, 'it's a very nice dress,' she added. Aimee was wearing an ivory long sleeve Bardot mini dress with high heel shoes, carrying a gold glitter envelope clutch bag.

'Thank you,' Aimee said with a smile, Lorraine held Aimee's hands and looked at her saying, 'I am really sorry I couldn't come to your nan's funeral; I was out of the country. June was a wonderful woman.' Aimee nodded her head and they hugged again.

'Would you like a glass of water?' Lorraine asked.

'Yes please,' Aimee replied, there was a pleasant aroma of rose & vanilla from the reed diffuser in fragrance in the hallway. Aimee followed Lorraine to the kitchen, Aimee could hear music "Thiago Silva" by Dave x AJ Tracey playing loudly from Matt's room upstairs.

Lorraine asked Aimee, 'How is your mum, is she doing well?' Aimee nodded.

'So, Matt tells me you have both decided to go to the same University, are you excited about that?' Lorraine asked, Aimee hesitated to respond. She had her mouth open but did not know what to say, Lorraine could sense Aimee was not comfortable with the question, so Lorraine thought to herself *It's not what she wants.* Aimee eventually responded,

'Yes,' but she said it with a low tone of voice.

'And is that what you want?' Lorraine asked, before Aimee could respond Lorraine moved forward and held Aimee's hand. 'If you don't agree with Matt, say it, tell him how you feel,' she said to Aimee.

A few seconds later Matt came downstairs and into the Kitchen, he saw his mum and girlfriend talking to each other, 'What lies is she feeding you Aimee?' he said. 'Let's go,' he added. Matt and Aimee were now walking to the party, twelve minutes into the walk they went into a quiet street, Aimee pulled Matt back by the hand, she held his hand and stopped walking, facing him.

Aimee said 'Matt, look, I need to talk to you,' she cleared her throat. 'I have been thinking about this for a while,' she paused as she was nervous. Aimee then added 'I have decided to go to Warwick Uni with Kat.'

'What? What the hell? That's far away, Coventry!?' he said surprised.

'Sorry, I should have told you earlier, its been on my mind.'

'We agreed on this, have you really thought it through?' Aimee nodded, Matt turned away from her, turned back to her and said, 'Do you know what you are doing to our relationship?'

'It's not like that,' Aimee responded,

'I care about you,' he put his arms around her waist and faced her, pulling her closer to him.

'I know, but it's my decision.'

'Which you made without me.'

'Matt your arms are too tight, move back,' Aimee said to him, she put her hand and clutch bag on his chest, gesturing to push him away, he released his arms, both at this point still standing on the pavement of the street.

Matt stood to Aimee's side leaning to her ear and said, 'Do you think you are going to have friends there?' he sniggered, and then moved back from her, and clasped his hands 'Even the two friends you have now don't have time for you,' he added.

'That's not true!' Aimee shook her head and walked away from Matt.

'Don't walk away from me,' he said to her.

'Matt, you keep putting me down, I am going home!'

'We're going to the party, what are you talking about?'

'I don't care about the party!'

'I have tried my best for you Aimee, for us, you're a waste of time!' he shouted.

There was a pause, Aimee turned round 'I saw you with Lucy!'

'Where?'

'At Morrisons'

Matt laughed, then put his hand over his mouth, 'Were you following me then?'

'No, I work there!' Aimee replied frustrated and emotional, her heart racing faster.

'What do you mean you work there, since when?'

'Don't change the subject!'

'You didn't tell me, so now who's being dishonest?'

'I saw you put your hands around her shoulder, both of you laughing, flirting.'

'Is that a crime now? You're off your head, nothing happened between me and Lucy!' Matt put his hands on his hips, 'but you know what, I wish it did, she is so much fun and knows how to have a good time, at least I laugh when I am with her,' he said to Aimee.

Aimee began sobbing, she walked off, heading back to the direction they came from, at the same time Kat rang Aimee who was now walking back home by herself, Aimee missed the phone call from Kat as her phone was on vibration mode, ringing in her clutch bag.

Aimee was upset. Instead of continuing to walk, she decided to get the bus home, she covered her mouth whilst sat on the bus, sobbing quietly. The bus was fairly empty, an older lady sat ahead of Aimee looked back at her, 'Are you alright love?' she asked, concerned.

'Yes, I am,' replied Aimee.

'It will be all right love,' said the old lady smiling, and Aimee smiled back.

Once Aimee arrived home, she went to her bedroom and sat on the bed thinking about herself and Matt. She kept thinking about all the times they had a fight an argument, how low it made her feel, she then opened her mobile phone and went to her Instagram account, she deleted the recent picture of herself and Matt, she wanted to delete more pictures but she paused. She got up from the bed and kneeled by her bed, she pulled out a white cardboard box from under her bed, she opened the top half of the box then removed a pair of high heeled shoes, she then unwrapped newspapers which were covering an item inside the box. Aimee looked at the door of her bedroom, she checked to make sure the door was closed properly, the unwrapped newspapers revealed an unfinished 1 litre bottle of Jack Daniels, Aimee opened the bottle, paused and then drank the remaining bottle.

It was now 8.56pm in the evening, Aimee's mobile phone vibrated with a received message from Kat saying *hope ure havin a gr8 time at the party x*. Kat had decided not to go to the party as she knew Matt would be there. When Aimee finished the bottle, she wanted to drink more and there was no alcohol in the Larkson household. She sat on the floor of her bedroom for a while, contemplating her life, she decided to find a bar or nightclub and go out alone.

Aimee still had her party dress on and put on her high heels, she ordered an Uber, she came downstairs to the hallway, put on a jacket to cover her dress, and left the house. Emma was in the living room, she heard the front door close, 'Aimee where are you going?' she asked but there was no response. She went to the living room window and saw Aimee getting into the Uber taxi, Aimee found a late-night bar and dancing venue in Crawley and the taxi dropped her off outside the nightclub.

Aimee approached the doorman, 'Alright love,' he said to her and she nodded as he opened the door and allowed her into the venue; the receptionist checked Aimee's ID.

Aimee went straight to the bar, 'Can I get a vodka shot,' she asked, after two vodka shots at the bar a young man approached Aimee, he spoke into her ear, 'Can I get you a drink?'

'Yes,' replied Aimee and he bought her a Jack Daniels and Coke which she drank with him. A few minutes later, Aimee was on the dance floor, the thump of the speakers vibrating through her body. She was in tune with the music, trying to forget all about Matt, closing her eyes dancing to forget the pain. "I'm A Slave 4 U" by Britney Spears was blasting through the speakers on the dance floor, the bass piercing though her eardrums. Aimee could feel and smell the sweat of the other dancers around her on the crowded dancefloor and as she opened her eyes, she saw a man making eye contact with her whilst dancing. He came forward smiling, tried to grab Aimee's hand and started dancing with her. Aimee tried to ignore him and moved away from him but there was limited space, she left the dancefloor and went back to the bar, ordering another shot.

The same man followed her to the bar, as Aimee was standing at the bar, he moved next to her and put his arms around her, Aimee moved away from him, 'Talk to me!' he shouted leaning into Aimee's ear, Aimee went to the toilet, she was trying to find her feet as she was losing her balance, she went into the cubicle and sat on the floor of the cubicle. Aimee brought out her mobile phone, hoping there would be a message from Matt, maybe even an apology, but there was nothing from him.

As Aimee sat on the floor of the cubicle in the nightclub toilets, she remembered what Matt had said to her a few months ago, that other guys wouldn't even look at her, that they wouldn't find her attractive. In her mind Aimee kept asking herself if this was true, if other boys would not find her attractive, she assured herself that it was not true and that she *could* still get the attention of the opposite sex.

Aimee left the toilets and went back to the dance floor; she noticed a young man dancing alone. She looked closely at his face to see how attractive he was. Aimee liked what she saw, she moved closer to him whilst dancing, and took him by the hand and she put her arms around him, around his back. He smiled at her, they danced together for eight more minutes maintaining eye contact, she leaned into his chest whilst they danced together. At this moment she thought to herself *I am still attractive*, he moved forward and kissed her, Aimee wanted to kiss him but suddenly she felt nauseous and dizzy, on the dancefloor there were revellers pushing against each other.

Aimee needed fresh air and she was sweating due to the heat from the nightclub, she walked away from the man she was dancing with, 'Where are you going?' he asked Aimee as she walked away. She went outside and walked a few metres before slumping against the side of the building. At this moment she received a WhatsApp message from Kat which was a love heart, no words just a love heart, when Aimee saw this she closed her eyes and was sad and put her head in her hands. A minute later she looked at her phone, specifically her wallpaper which was a picture of herself and Matt, she wanted to call Matt, she dialled his number then cancelled the call, changing her mind. Kat called her best friend again; she hadn't heard from Aimee all night and was getting worried but, because Aimee was feeling nauseous, she did not pick up the call.

Kat was at home in the maisonette flat in Reigate, which her uncle paid the rent for. It was the early hours of Sunday morning, 1.04 am, and Kat was lying down on the sofa in the living room, with her girlfriend Yas next to her on the sofa. Kat was in a spooning position with her, Yas was in her underwear and wearing Kat's t-shirt, Kat was in her own pyjamas. The television was still on as they had fallen asleep, the living room lights were off.

Kat and Yas both heard a knock on the front door of the flat, 'Who is that?' Yas asked Kat yawning.

Yas put on her jeans which were on the living room floor, Kat got up from the sofa and went to the front door, she could hear that it was raining outside, she opened the front door and saw Aimee. Kat was concerned to see Aimee was in tears, her hair wet from the rain and her arms crossed as it was cold. 'Oh my god Aimz, what's wrong? Come in,' she said to Aimee, Yas sighed once she heard Aimee's name from the living room.

Aimee said to Kat, 'I'm sorry,' as she stood in the hallway, her clothes wet from the rain, 'I just needed to ......' Aimee paused she looked to the floor then suddenly she ran to the bathroom and vomited. Yas came out of the living room with her arms crossed as Kat followed Aimee to the bathroom, Aimee was slumped over the toilet. Kat put her hand on Aimee's back, rubbing her back slowly, Aimee then sat on the bathroom floor with her back against the radiator.

Yas was not impressed and started to bite on the inside of her mouth as she leaned against the wall by the living room, 'Let's get you to the bedroom,' Kat said to Aimee, kneeling down to her level and putting her hand on Aimee's shoulder.

'No I'm fine,' Aimee responded.

'No, you're not', Kat walked with Aimee to the bedroom, she got her best friend out of the wet clothes and gave Aimee spare pyjamas. She also gave Aimee a dry towel for her wet hair, Aimee sneezed. Kat sat by the bed, Aimee laid on the bed and looked up at the ceiling.

'I feel like my life is falling apart, I've messed it all up,' she said.

'It will be ok, now rest, here, drink some water,' Kat gave Aimee a glass of water which was on the bedside table.

Aimee covered herself with the duvet, Kat got up from the bedside and switched off the bedside lamp, within minutes Aimee started to drift into sleep.

When Kat came out of the bedroom and closed the door, she saw disappointment on Yas's face, her lips were clenched together, Yas walked back to the living room.

Kat followed her, 'Are you done?' Yas asked Kat.

'Sorry, she's just had too much to drink……. I am right here,' Kat replied putting her arms around Yas's waist and looking into her eyes.

'How long is she going to stay?'

'Just for the night,'

'She doesn't need a babysitter,' Yas sighed, 'I don't like what happened last time she was around, when we were at Lewis's party, you just abandoned me to deal with her drama.'

'She is my friend.'

'I don't need this, I'm leaving,' Yas shook her head. Kat followed Yas, who picked up her leather jacket and headed to the front door to open it. Kat put her hand on the door handle to stop Yas from leaving, she closed the door and faced Yas.

Yas had her back to the door, Kat moved closer to her, Kat placed her hands on Yas's face and kissed her, 'I am here,' Kat said to Yas softly. Kat moved her left hand under Yas's top, moving her fingers over her navel and proceeded to kiss her slowly.

Yas put her arms around Kat's neck and they were kissing intensely. Yas dropped her leather jacket to the floor, Kat held Yas's wrists upwards above her head and against the door, she started to kiss Yas on her neck, Yas had her mouth open enjoying the kisses on her neck, Kat then dropped to her knee slowly whilst looking up at Yas, she started to unbutton and unzip the front of Yas' jeans, resting her face on Yas's navel, she kissed her below her belly button tenderly. Yas was leaning up against the front door, her jeans fell to the floor, Kat started to pull down Yas's underwear, then suddenly they both heard Aimee retching upstairs. Yas sighed, pulled up her jeans, picked up her leather jacket, zipped up her jacket and jeans, she opened the front door and left. Kat went outside in her pyjamas, following Yas. it was raining, Kat ran in front of Yas and held her hand before she got to the street, 'we're having such a good time,' Kat said to her.

There was a pause.

'Let me know when you stop babysitting,' Yas replied and walked off.

Kat went back into the flat and closed the front door, she leaned with her back against the front door and sighed, she went to the bedroom to check on Aimee. Aimee was back in bed and resting, Kat then brought out her mobile phone, she sent a text message to Emma letting her know that Aimee was safe and staying with her for the night.

Kat took off her pyjamas and laid in the bed next to Aimee, Kat still had her underwear on. She looked at Aimee as she slept, Kat opened her phone and sent Yas a WhatsApp message: *plz come back.*

There was no response from Yas for a few minutes, Kat kept WhatsApp open, then saw the notification.

Yas is typing ......

But there was no response from Yas, Yas chose not to respond, Kat sent another message.

At least please let me know when you get home

Kat stayed up for another 27 minutes, looking at pictures on her phone gallery of herself and Yas, Kat eventually fell asleep next to Aimee.

In the morning, Aimee woke up. As her eyes opened, she saw the sunlight shining through the window in the bedroom, she squinted her eyes as she raised her head from the pillow, and wiped the drool of spit from one side of her face which ran unto the pillow.

She turned to the other side of the bed to see Kat sitting by the bedside, smiling at her, and presenting her with a cup of tea. Aimee sat up in the bed, took the cup of tea, rested her back against the pillows and headboard.

'Where is Yas?' Aimee asked, Kat looked down at the bedroom floor.

'She left.'

'I'm really sorry.'

'It's ok.'

Kat got up and opened the bedroom window, she looked back at Aimee and said, 'I don't know what this is Aimz, but this isn't you.'

Aimee replied, 'I just wanted to forget everything,' she put her head in her hand whilst holding the cup of tea, Kat took a deep breath.

'I've been there trust me this is not the way,' Kat moved to Aimee's bedside and leaned down to give Aimee a hug, 'I love you so much,' she said to Aimee, there was a pause.

Kat added, 'You need to call your mum, she's been worried.'

Five days later, Saturday, the day of Karis's wedding had arrived. The night before, Emma drove from Reigate, Surrey to Moreton-In-Marsh, Gloucestershire, bringing with her Aimee and Kat as passengers.

They were staying at The Manor House Hotel, the hotel grounds were the setting for the wedding. Emma stayed in a deluxe double room, Kat and Aimee stayed together in a double room. They checked in on Friday evening.

The Stowell family were there to support Karis on her wedding day, mum, dad, and her younger brother Leyton.

During the afternoon the weather was perfect; clear blue skies with the sun shining and a 23-degree heat. All the guests were sat down to eat, it was 4.45pm, the starter and main course were about to be served to the wedding guests. All the guests were in their best attire for the wedding. Emma was wearing a long sleeve exposed bra maxi dress in dark green, Aimee was wearing a pale pink silk floral dress. Kat was wearing a knee length sleeveless navy-blue dress with white floral prints. Prior to the guests sitting for lunch, Karis had seen Kat and Aimee briefly and was delighted they could make it.

Emma, Kat and Aimee were sat at table four of fourteen round tables in the dining hall. In the hall was the sound of chatter the guests talking to each other, the tables were laid out perfectly, a white cloth over each table, a huge floral bouquet in the middle of the table in a glass vase, a wine glass, a champagne glass; gold stainless steel cutlery, white round porcelain plates with a gold rim, beneath the porcelain plates were larger gold dinner plates, on the tables were also white cloth napkins tied in a gold ribbon.

Emma left her mobile phone on the table as she got up to use the toilet. Aimee was talking to Kat who was sat next to her, a second later a WhatsApp message came up on the screen of Emma's phone, Aimee had just glanced at Emma's phone for a second and saw the WhatsApp message clearly displayed on the phone screen,

I have missed tasting you ….

Aimee covered her mouth in shock, she didn't recognize the number and it wasn't Jerome's number, she looked over to Kat with her eyes wide open in surprise, 'Are you ok?' Kat asked.

'Yeeeeeeessss,' Aimee said slowly,

'Something you want to tell me?'

'No, nothing,' Kat and Aimee continued to talk but all that kept running through Aimee's mind was who could have sent that message to Emma?

Half an hour later Leyton came to table four, he was in a tailored navy three-piece suit with a white long sleeve cotton shirt under the suit, also wearing cufflinks and a tie. He gave Aimee and Kat a hug and was delighted to see them. Kat, Aimee, and Leyton talked for a while at the table. Emma had left the table, Aimee noticed her mum had to take a call and had been speaking to a mystery person on the phone. she was curious to know if Emma was speaking to the same person that sent that surprising message.

A few more hours had passed at the wedding celebrations, it was 8.51pm, the dancefloor was already open and the party guests were enjoying the music. Kat, Leyton and Karis were dancing the "electric slide" in synchronicity with everyone on the dancefloor, the song playing was "Candy" by Cameo. Whilst dancing Karis glanced to see that Aimee's wasn't smiling, she saw Aimee sat by herself at the table.

Aimee had just received a WhatsApp message from Matt *are you missing me* , with the message he also attached a selfie of himself with his shirt off and open chest whilst sat in bed. Karis took a quick break from dancing, she left the dancefloor and went to Aimee, 'Come' she said to Aimee, and she took Aimee aside to talk to her. Karis put her arms around Aimee's waist, she said to Aimee, 'I can see something is on your mind,' Aimee flicked her hair backward and broke eye contact with Karis, she then looked at Karis. Karis added, 'It's Matt that is on your mind, am I wrong?'

Aimee sighed, Karis took Aimee's hand and said to her, 'Today was the day I decided to be with and marry my life long partner, I am only going to say this, if you don't see Matt as the one for you the don't settle,' she released Aimee's hand and then put her hand on Aimee's shoulder. 'I am back from honeymoon the week after next, just call me if you ever want to talk Aimee,' Aimee nodded her head, they hugged.

Aimee left the party and headed back to the hotel room to be alone, 23 minutes later Kat realised she couldn't see Aimee. Kat looked around the dancefloor, the dining tables, the bar, she looked outside in the gardens, she could not find Aimee, she called Aimee but there was no response.

Aimee was in the bathroom, she left her phone on the bed as soon as she came back to the hotel room, she looked at herself in the mirror, memories of her relationship with Matt were going through her mind, the times she kissed him, held him, laughed with him, the times he told her he loved her.

Aimee's mascara was running, Kat came into the hotel room, she used her key card to get in, she heard the tap running in the bathroom, Aimee left the tap running as she did not want Kat to know she was upset. Kat put her ear to the door, she could hear Aimee sniffing. She could sense Aimee had been crying, 'Aimz are you ok? Please don't cry,' she said through the door. Aimee took a deep breath, the bathroom door opened, Kat and Aimee looked each other in the eye and they hugged.

Kat put her hand on Aimee's hair and Aimee closed her eyes, Aimee shook her head, stepped back from the hug, opened her eyes and said to Kat, 'It's because of you I have found it hard to enjoy being with Matt, you have never accepted him, you have never given him a chance.'

Kat groaned in frustration, her eyes opened wider, 'Oh my god are you fucking...., are you for real right now Aimee?!' there was a pause, 'I have been bending over backwards to tolerate him for you, for our friendship,' Kat added, Aimee was motionless with a blank stare. Kat put her hands on her hips, she looked to the floor and shook her head, 'Aimee don't do this, don't push me away,' she said to her best friend. Kat's bottom lip started to quiver.

Aimee looked to the ceiling and started to hyperventilate, 'I don't know what to do, I am scared I will be alone forever Kat,' Aimee said crying, Kat held her hand.

Aimee sat down on the bed, Kat said to her, 'Just breathe, take a deep breath, I am right here,' Kat put her hand behind Aimee's back whilst sitting next to her on the bed. Aimee had her head in her hands, there was a pause, Aimee said with a low voice 'I have this feeling, eventually everyone I care about will leave me.'

'No, we all love you,' replied Kat. Aimee went to the bathroom, she took off her outfit for the wedding and her underwear, she stepped into the shower; she came out of the shower 8 minutes later in a bathrobe. When Aimee came out of the bathroom, she saw Kat sitting on the bed watching television and said to Kat, 'I am sorry, go and enjoy the rest of the party, I know you want to.'

Kat smiled and shook her head, 'I am ok here, I want to make sure you are ok,' she said to Aimee.

A few minutes later, Kat changed into her pyjamas, Kat and Aimee were sat on the bed next to each other, with their back against the pillows. Aimee took Kat's hand and said to her, 'I hope you make it; I hope you go all the way,'

'With what?'

'Acting, on stage, on tv, all of it, you're so alive when you're acting, captivating, and I will be there, front row as your number 1 fan to any play or show you're in,' Kat smiled.

'Well, I am very proud of you aimz, despite everything you have been through, you still have so much warmth and love to give, your determination, your desire to live life is still there, I respect you for that.'

Kat and Aimee continued talking and two hours later both fell asleep together.

The next day, Sunday morning, Emma, Kat, and Aimee checked out of the hotel, Emma drove back to Surrey with Aimee and Kat.

JULY

It was 4.03pm on a hot Saturday afternoon in July, Aimee and Kat were preparing to go to Brighton, East Sussex for a concert. They picked up their train tickets from the ticket machine outside Reigate train station; their plan was to get on the Great Western Rail train from Reigate, Surrey to Gatwick Airport and change at Gatwick to get another train, either the Southern Train or Thameslink from Gatwick Airport station to Brighton.

On the first part of the journey, they sat towards the middle of the Great Western Rail train, smiling as they sat opposite each other, Kat put her feet up on the seat next to Aimee. You could hear the noise of the train as it started to pull away from

Platform 1 at Reigate station, and through the train windows you could feel the heat from the sun which was shining brightly. There were a few other passengers sat around Kat and Aimee in the same train coach.

Kat and Aimee were eating and talking on the train, sharing popcorn, about two minutes into the train journey after departing Reigate station, Kat's ex-girlfriend Yas was walking down the train towards the back of the train, Yas was walking with a friend behind her, she saw Kat sat down, and ignored her, choosing to look ahead whilst walking, Yas was wearing a short white crop top, denim midi skirt, a choker and trainers.

Kat looked up and noticed Yas, Kat sat upright in her seat and flicked her hair back, 'Hi Yas,' Kat said with a slight smile looking up at her and hoping for a response. Yas ignored her and continued to walk further down the train to the last carriage, in that moment as Yas walked past Kat, Kat took in a breath of Yas's perfume and the intimate moments she had with Yas during their relationship flooded back, the holding of hands, kissing her lips, kissing her neck, wearing her clothes, lying next to her.

'Was that Yas?' Aimee asked surprised, Kat nodded her head and bit her lip, Kat took a deep breath in, she blushed but was smiling awkwardly, and looked outside the train window feeling embarrassed.

For the duration of the train journey after seeing Yas, Kat hardly spoke or smiled, she kept thinking of how the relationship ended with Yas, the train arrived at Gatwick Airport train station, as Kat and Aimee got up, the train doors opened and they stepped onto the platform. Yas also came off the train at Gatwick Airport train station. Yas walked to the opposite platform waiting for trains toward Brighton, Yas looked back at Kat, and Kat quickly diverted her eyes away whilst stood next to Aimee on the platform.

Aimee stood in front of Kat, she put her hand on Kat's arm, 'Go and talk to her,'

Aimee said to Kat. Kat shook her head and cleared her throat but kept facing away from Yas.

The train to Brighton arrived on the opposite platform, Yas stepped onto the Brighton train, 'She's getting on the same train,' Kat said to Aimee.

'So what? Come on,' Aimee said pulling Kat by the arm, they decided to board the Brighton train, which was still on the platform, they avoided going into the part of the train that Yas was in.

Half an hour later the train arrived at Brighton station, Kat and Aimee walked through the ticket barriers and exited the station. In the heat of the sun, they walked to the Brighton Centre, the venue of the concert they were attending, they walked down Queens Road and West Street.

5.32pm Kat and Aimee decided to get food before the concert and went to Brighton Palace Pier fish and chip shop by the beach, they sat next to each other and ate on Brighton beach, watching the sun, hearing the sound of the seagulls, the sound of the waves, the sound of children and adults around them.

Kat laughed at Aimee, 'What's funny?' Aimee asked, as they were eating, there was mayonnaise on Aimee's face, and on the side of her mouth. Kat put her finger on the mayonnaise which was on the side of Aimee lips and licked her finger.

'It's good to see you smiling,' Aimee said to Kat. She added, 'You've been very quiet ever since we ran into Yas'.

'I have to admit I wasn't prepared for seeing her again,' Kat replied, there was a pause. She added, 'but I have noticed a change in you recently though, more freedom, you seem happier, well certainly happier compared to last month,' she said to Aimee.

Kat took Aimee by the hand and looked at her, 'And you deserve that, to be happy, I know the breakup with Matt was................ difficult,' Aimee broke eye contact and looked forward at the waves.

Kat moved to sit opposite her best friend

and held both of Aimee's hands, 'You have your whole life ahead of you and every step of the way I will always be there, I promise.' Aimee smiled, and they hugged whilst sat down.

As Kat and Aimee sat on the pebbled shore, Kat looked at Aimee and said to her, 'I need to admit something, sometimes I am jealous of you Aimz. You have a brilliant step dad who loves you so much, you have Emma who has always got your back.' Kat put her food down to her side, she looked down at the pebbles in front of her, shook her head and took a breath to compose herself, holding back her emotions, she added, 'and I wish I had a mum like her and a house that feels like home,' Kat's voice broke as she said this.

Aimee put her hand on Kat's back,

'What I would give to be in a house filled with happy memories,' Kat said to Aimee, she wiped a tear from her eye, 'All the memories that live with me in that flat are of pain and regret, I live with all those memories, my mum and my relationships are a train wreck,' Kat added.

'But Kat you have lots of friends, I've never told you this, but I envy you for that,' Aimee replied.

'Just because you know plenty of people, doesn't mean they will be there for you, doesn't mean they know what you're actually going through.'

Aimee gave Kat a tissue, to wipe the tears on her face.

There was a pause for a few minutes.

Kat looked out towards the sea and said, 'I want us to travel the world Aimee, see every continent, experience many cultures before we are 30.'

Aimee smiled. 'I would love that, Nan would have loved to join us. I really miss her.'

It was now 6.42pm, Kat and Aimee left the beach, they walked to the Brighton Centre, the doors of the concert they were attending were meant to open at 7pm. After queuing at the entrance, they passed security, the doors to the floor of the Brighton Centre opened, Kat ran in excitement to the front of the stage. Kat and Aimee took a picture of themselves with the stage behind them and then sent it to Leyton.

Whilst Aimee and Kat waited for the concert to start, the arena started to fill up, people were coming into the West Balcony, East Balcony, South Balcony and floor standing. Kat noticed Yas standing a few meters away from her with a friend. 8.00pm, the house lights of the Brighton Centre were dimmed, then turned off and it became dark in the arena, the concert had started. Kat and Aimee started to scream in excitement, all around them were fans also screaming, including those standing and seating in the stalls, the atmosphere was electric, the lights and the thump of the speakers, Kat and Aimee were at the concert in complete ecstasy holding each other, song after song they were singing together.

Towards the end of the concert, Kat embraced Aimee from behind, putting her arms around Aimee's waist and resting her chin on her shoulder. Kat kissed Aimee's shoulder, they sang to "Secret Love Song" by Little Mix word for word at the top of their lungs. Aimee was waving her phone in the air slowly with the torch mode on, there was a sea of white lights across the arena as everyone held up their phone. Aimee let out a little scream in excitement when a member of the group on stage stood before her, waved and smiled at her.

10.15pm the concert had finished, Aimee and Kat left the concert venue and were standing opposite PRYZM Nightclub, 'Let me check the trains,' Kat said to Aimee, she brought out her phone, 'there is a train to Gatwick Airport at 10.25,' said Kat, 'the other trains seem to be cancelled' she added.

'Let's just get a taxi,' Aimee responded.

'No, we can make it if we leave now, we can walk,' Kat replied, Aimee sighed.

They started to walk up West Street

towards Brighton train station, 'Let's walk as fast as we can,' Kat said, three minutes into walking Aimee stopped.

'I have a stitch,' she said laughing, she stooped over holding her belly.

'We have to make the last train come on!' said Kat.

'Let's just get a taxi,' Aimee replied, they ran for their last train leaving Brighton heading to Gatwick Airport, the plan was to then take a train from Gatwick to Reigate. Kat was ahead, she ran into Brighton train station, then ran past the ticket barriers, onto the platform. Aimee was a few seconds behind her. 'Quickly!' Kat shouted at Aimee, the alarm of the closing train doors went off, they started to beep to signal they were closing, 'Aaaaah !' Aimee shrieked, Kat stood between the train doors, Aimee leaped from the platform into the train through a small gap whilst the doors were closing, the doors closed, and they both fell over on the floor of the train laughing.

'You're such a liability,' Kat said to Aimee

jokingly, Aimee couldn't respond, she was out of breath. She stooped down trying to breathe, Kat found a seat nearby, Aimee joined her, she sat down, some of her hair clumped to her face due to sweat. A few minutes later Aimee started to fall asleep on Kat's shoulder.

Several days had passed, it was Friday evening, Aimee and Kat had just finished calling each other, they agreed to meet the next day which was a Saturday. 11.21pm that Friday evening, Aimee lay on her bed looking up at the ceiling, she received a notification from her mobile phone that her device storage space was low, she decided to delete some photos and videos to save storage space, she went through the pictures of herself and Kat on her phone. Hundreds of them, scrolling through them, she was smiling as she looked at each picture, half an hour later, Aimee turned to her side ready to go to bed, she covered herself with the duvet, her head relaxed on the pillow, she then sent a love heart message to Kat on WhatsApp, Kat responded the same within seconds.

Aimee put her phone down on the bedside table, as she was lying down, she thought of the time Kat kissed her shoulder at the concert. She thought about the feeling of holding Kat's hand as they walked on Brighton beach, she turned off the bedside lamp to sleep.

Within twelve minutes she fell asleep and later whilst asleep started to dream, in her dream she saw:

Kat in a white bath robe sitting by the beach, there was no one else on the beach, the clear blue sea ahead of her, the waves coming up to Kat's feet. Kat smiled at Aimee and gestured her to come over, Aimee tried to move forward to get closer to Kat but couldn't, she felt herself unable to move her legs, she looked down into the sand, she could see her feet but couldn't move them. She looked up and she called for Kat but Aimee could not hear her own voice, she then felt someone grab her arm from behind, she turned around to see who was holding her, it was Matt. Matt looked at her with a blank expression, he was wearing a grey suit and black roll neck jumper, she looked at him and she couldn't move, she was afraid. Her feet began to sink into the sand, she then turned away, looking back towards Kat for help. Kat got up and started to walk towards Aimee, Kat separated Matt's hands from Aimee's arm, then they were walking together towards the waves on the beach.

At this point Aimee woke up from her dream, she checked the time on her phone saw it was 2.31am, before going back to sleep.

Upon waking up at 8.22am on Saturday morning, Aimee turned to her bedside table, she drank from her glass of water, which was on the table, she reached for her phone and sent a WhatsApp message to Kat.

Aimee: *meet me at the cinema today*

Kat: *around 7?*

Aimee: *my shift finishes at 7pm*

Kat: *which one?*

Aimee: *what do you mean?*

Kat: *which cinema?*

Aimee: *Odeon Epsom*

Kat: *ok*

It was the evening, 8.02pm, Aimee had finished work, she was waiting for Kat outside the Odeon cinema, Aimee was wearing a white crop top with blue floral prints and ripped high waisted white denim shorts. She was listening to music with her earphones, "Shivers" by Ed Sheeran playing into her ears. She went next door to Costa Coffee, after looking at the menu, she ordered a Peach Hibiscus iced tea to go, as she stepped outside, she saw Kat walking down the high street.

Aimee and Kat met at the front of Odeon cinema in Epsom, they embraced each other. Kat was wearing a grey Guns n Roses t-shirt with navy-blue denim shorts. They proceeded to the escalator inside the building of the cinema, Kat was calm and relaxed, but Aimee was excited, she hugged Kat from behind, smiling and placing her chin on Kat's shoulders as they moved up the escalators. Kat looked over her shoulder smiling briefly. Aimee liked the familiarity of being close to her best friend, holding her, the smell of Kat's t-shirt, the feeling of Kat's t-shirt on her cheek. They approached the food and drinks counter at the cinema, Aimee was looking at Kat and was cheerful, the cashier asked, 'How can I help?' Aimee responded, 'Can we have one mixed popcorn, two large nachos with everything please?'

'Sure, and what drink would you like?'

'Sprite,' Kat and Aimee said at the same time, then smiled.

'Coming right up,' said the cashier. Kat leaned on the counter and looked at Aimee and squinted her eyes saying, 'There is something different about you, have you been drinking?'

'What? No Just happy to be here.' They paid for the refreshments, collected their cinema tickets, took their food and drinks with them.

Aimee and Kat walked into Screen 3 together to watch the movie; they had arrived early to the screening and took their seats a few rows from the front. Aimee went to the toilet and five minutes later came back to her seat, 25 minutes later the adverts and trailers had finished showing and the lights in Screen 3 were dimmed, the movie started.

Aimee couldn't pay attention to the film, her eyes were darting left and right as thoughts were running through her mind, a few minutes into the film she felt this warmth that came over her, from her head down to her chest, her heart was beating faster, she felt that at this moment she needed to speak to Kat. Aimee leaned towards Kat and put her hand on Kat's thigh, 'Come with me,' she whispered into Kat's ear, Kat looked at her and said,

'The film has just started,' Aimee stood up from her seat and looked at Kat, she took Kat's hand, 'What are you doing?' Kat asked whispering. Kat put the nachos that were on her lap on the floor, she stood up from her seat, they left their drinks, food and bag at the seats. They walked to the side exit of Screen 3, it was dark however they could see the fire exit sign and the exit door, they came out of Screen 3 through the doors, Aimee still holding Kat by the hand took her to the next Screen, Screen 4, they opened the doors and entered Screen 4 to find the seats filled with people and a movie showing, Aimee took Kat out of Screen 4. Kat stopped, 'Ok what are you up to?' she asked Aimee whispering, Aimee gently put her finger on Kat's lips. She then took Kat by the hand and led her into Screen 5, when they walked into Screen 5 it was quiet and empty.

'Aimee, what are you up to?' Kat asked smiling, Aimee walked in front of the giant screen, the projector was off, no images were displayed on the screen, the lights in the ceiling were dimly lit with a blue glow, there was complete silence.

They stood in the middle of Screen 5 on

the carpeted floor, Aimee faced Kat and held both her hands, Aimee closed her eyes and took a deep breath, she opened her eyes. 'Please just listen,' she said to Kat, there was a pause, Kat nodded.

Aimee said to her, 'I've been thinking about what I want in my life, who makes me happy, feel free, excited, the only person I think of ….' Aimee swallowed to clear her throat, 'the only person I think about when I am happy is you, I trust you and you have always been there for me, you are genuine, I love how you make me feel………. I love you Kat.' When Aimee said the "L" word her voice broke, she looked up to the ceiling and took a deep breath, then she looked back at Kat, Kat put her right hand on Aimee's left cheek to wipe away a tear, Kat immediately hugged Aimee, then Kat started to cry as they hugged.

After they hugged, Kat and Aimee stood in front of each other, still holding hands, 'I love you,' Kat said to Aimee. Aimee could feel her heart racing, she leaned forward slowly, tilted her head slightly and kissed Kat on the mouth, Kat reciprocated, Aimee suddenly had a feeling of warmth in her upper body, Kat put her arms around Aimee's waist as they kissed, Aimee put the palm of her hands on Kat's cheeks. Kat moved her head back, she put her lips together, 'Are you sure this is what you want?' she asked Aimee.

'Yes,' Aimee replied looking to Kat's eyes, they continued kissing slowly, Kat started to kiss Aimee on her cheek, moving towards her ears. Aimee could feel Kat's warm breath in her ear, Kat then took Aimee by the hand and moved to sit on a seat in the front row.

Aimee sat across her lap, they continued kissing, they paused, 'I don't know what I am feeling right now, I'm excited and nervous at the same time,' Aimee said to Kat.

'That's ok' said Kat, Aimee rested her face on Kat's face, their foreheads touching, their noses touching, they could hear and feel each other's breath. Aimee put her fingers on Kat's neck, caressing her neck, they were kissing passionately, Kat moved tongue further forward into Aimee's mouth as they kissed, she wrapped her arms tightly around Aimee. Aimee took her hand and placed it under Kat's t-shirt, on her chest whilst they kissed, suddenly they heard the doors to Screen 5 open and chatter as people started to walk into Screen 5.

Aimee quickly got up from Kat's lap, Kat got up from the front row seat, they both left Screen 5 holding hands. Kat went back to Screen 3 to pick up their personal belongings. She came out of Screen 3 and met Kat by the entrance, they kissed briefly.

'What should we do?' Aimee asked.

'Anything you want,' said Kat smiling.

After leaving the cinema, the sun had started to set. Aimee and Kat took the 460 bus from Epsom to Reigate, the bus stopped close to the road where Kat lives by herself. They got off the bus and walked to Hadley Court, a block of Maisonette

Flats. Kat used her key to open the front door, they both took their trainers off, and they went to the kitchen, Kat fetched a glass of water with ice for Aimee and for herself, a glass of lemonade with ice.

Kat walked ahead of Aimee and opened the bedroom door, Aimee also walked into the bedroom, Kat switched on both bedside lamps, which gave the room a warm glow.

Kat's bedroom had brilliant white walls, with navy blue curtains to the side of the window and a dark grey carpet flooring, a small built in mirrored wardrobe to the side of the room and her bed in the middle of the room, there was also a desk and above the desk on the wall were pictures of herself with Aimee, Leyton, friends and her uncle, these pictures were all over the wall above the desk.

A "Romeo + Juliet" movie poster was on the wall to the right of the desk, Kat had a sip of her drink and put the glass down on the bedside table, they both sat at the bedside. Aimee drank her glass of water slowly, lowered it, she leaned towards the bedside table and put down the glass of water.

Aimee moved to sit in the middle of Kat's bed with her legs crossed, she took off her crop top and looked at Kat, she held Kat's hand, Kat moved closer and sat behind Aimee on the bed. Kat put her fingers on the back of Aimee's neck, caressing her, moving her fingers down slowly towards the back of Aimee's bra. Aimee turned her head to look back at Kat, 'Go ahead,' she said to Kat, Kat put her fingers together to undo Aimee's bra, Aimee's bra dropped, Kat put her arms across Aimee's chest and slowly wrapped her legs around Aimee's waist.

She held Aimee's hair away from the back of her neck and to one side, she started to kiss the back of her neck, Kat tilted her head, leaned forward and kissed Aimee on the side of her neck whilst holding Aimee's hands. Kat then lowered her head and slowly kissed Aimee on the shoulder. Aimee closed her eyes taking in the moment.

Whilst sat on the bed, Aimee turned to face Kat and they looked at each other, eye to eye, there was a pause, they kissed, Aimee derived pleasure from kissing Kat, the softness of Kat's lips, the taste of her mouth, the comfort, the familiarity, the passion. Kat leaned backwards onto the bed, her head resting on the pillow, Aimee put her hands on Kat's navy-blue denim shorts, feeling the texture of the denim. She unbuttoned the shorts whilst making eye contact with Kat, Aimee pulled down and took off the denim shorts, throwing them to the floor. Aimee then kneeled on the bed and removed her ripped white denim shorts.

They laid on the bed next to each other, facing each other, the palm of Aimee's hand placed gently on Kat's face, Kat put her hand through Aimee's hair, they continued to kiss.

Kat took the duvet and put it over both of them, Aimee then laid back on the bed, under the duvet, her head resting against the pillow, she took a deep breath, Kat moved between Aimee's thigh, she took the time to kiss Aimee's inner thigh, Aimee's mouth was open as she received pleasure from every kiss Kat placed on her body.

Kat moved her head upwards; she faced Aimee and asked her, 'Do you want me to continue?'

'Yes,' replied Aimee, Aimee put her lips together, she placed her finger on Kat's lips feeling the shape of her lips. Kat moved back downwards under the duvet, she pulled off Aimee's underwear, Kat proceeded to go down on Aimee, thrusting her lips forward tightly between Aimee's legs. Aimee gasped clutching the bedsheet, Kat used one of her hands to hold Aimee's upper thigh, she placed her other hand on Aimee's breast, then using her finger caressed Aimee's nipple. Aimee was breathing heavily, she started to moan lounder as Kat used her tongue expertly.

Kat took pleasure in using her fingers, her mouth, her lips, her tongue to please Aimee, after several minutes of giving Aimee oral pleasure, Aimee started to shudder, her heart palpitating. Kat's heart was also racing, Aimee clutched the bedsheet intensely, she let out a huge moan, she climaxed and breathed out heavily.

There was a pause, as Kat moved up the bed and smiled at Aimee. Aimee smiled back at her and licked the inside of her lips, they kissed. Aimee was sweating, some of her hair clumped to her face, they laid down opposite each other as they continued to kiss into the night, eventually falling asleep together.

SEPTEMBER

The 2nd of September, it was raining heavily in the afternoon with grey skies, there was a smell of wet leaves and wet grass. Kat and Aimee both stood in front of a grave holding hands. Kat held up a black umbrella over herself and Aimee with her other hand. Aimee was standing next to Kat, they were at Epsom Memorial Cemetery, the grave they stood in front of had a headstone, it read "PHIL LARKSON BELOVED FATHER, HUSBAND AND FRIEND. 1980 TO 2014". There was a pause, a tear dropped from Aimee's eye as she looked at the headstone, 'I miss you dad,' Aimee whispered, she walked forward to place flowers at the headstone and stepped back.

Kat was wearing a grey oversized hooded jumper and grey joggers; Aimee was wearing a white long sleeve turtleneck top with a navy blue puffer coat over it and denim jeans.

After ten minutes they walked out of the cemetery and park together, Kat put her left hand around Aimee's back, and was still holding the umbrella with her other hand, they were unaware someone was watching them, Matt was watching Kat and Aimee from afar. He stood behind one of the trees in the park which was opposite the cemetery, he was wearing a black hoodie and black joggers with trainers, as he stepped forward, he took his hoodie down and leaned on the tree nearby, his eyes fixed on Kat and Aimee. He brought out his mobile phone, accessed his camera app, zoomed in to take a picture of Kat and Aimee at the precise moment they kissed whilst walking.

A few minutes, later Kat and Aimee were on the bus taking them back to Reigate town centre, they sat next to each other towards the back of the bus. Kat placed her hand on Aimee's right thigh, Aimee was looking at the locket Jerome gave her with the picture of her and her dad inside it, she closed her eyes and took in a deep breath. Kat looked at her and said, 'Whatever happens, you have me, I will always be here.'

'I know,' Aimee responded with a smile, and they kissed.

THE END

Printed in Dunstable, United Kingdom